...ven't give...
What if you sh... ...a different
'wife' later?"

"You've decided."

His confidence irked her—and pleased her. Denise liked that he had that much sense of himself.

Gideon plucked the ring from the box and held it up. "Want to see if it fits?"

She held out her hand. The ring seemed on fire, as if chiding her for telling a lie by pretending to be married. "It's fine," she said, then tugged it off immediately and handed it back to him. "Did you get one for yourself?"

"I did. It's plain." Instead of tucking the ring back in the box, he pulled out a tissue-wrapped packet that contained a long silver chain. He slipped her ring onto it, lifted it over her head and let it dip inside her blouse.

She felt it slide into her cleavage then nestle.

"For when you're not playing the part," he said, kissing her lightly on the lips.

Dear Reader,

One of the things I love most about connected books is the pleasure of revisiting the characters from the other stories. In my WIVES FOR HIRE series, it's the Falcon brothers of Chance City, California, a fictional small town in the Sierra foothills.

While each book in this series is first and foremost about a man and woman finding their perfect life mate—and all the magic and beauty that journey entails—it's also about having brothers and what that means, too. Siblings share a unique bond and are a different kind of life mate. Creating moments for David, Noah and Gideon Falcon to interact was a great deal of fun for me, and a loving tribute to my own brothers.

So, this book is about family—the one you're born into and the one you create when you marry. Both are meant to be treasured.

Susan

THE
MILLIONAIRE'S
CHRISTMAS WIFE

SUSAN CROSBY

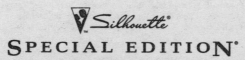

SPECIAL EDITION

Published by Silhouette Books

America's Publisher of Contemporary Romance

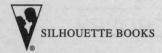 SILHOUETTE BOOKS

ISBN-13: 978-0-373-24936-7
ISBN-10: 0-373-24936-5

THE MILLIONAIRE'S CHRISTMAS WIFE

Visit Silhouette Books at www.eHarlequin.com

Printed in U.S.A.

Books by Susan Crosby

Silhouette Special Edition

*The Bachelor's Stand-In Wife #1912
**The Rancher's Surprise Marriage #1922
*The Single Dad's Virgin Wife #1930
*The Millionaire's Christmas Wife #1936

Silhouette Desire

†Christmas Bonus, Strings Attached #1554
†Private Indiscretions #1570
†Hot Contact #1590
†Rules of Attraction #1647
†Heart of the Raven #1653
†Secrets of Paternity #1659
The Forbidden Twin #1717
Forced to the Altar #1733
Bound by the Baby #1797

*Wives for Hire
**Back in Business
†Behind Closed Doors

SUSAN CROSBY

believes in the value of setting goals, but also in the magic of making wishes, which often do come true—as long as she works hard enough. Along life's journey she's done a lot of the usual things—married, had children, attended college a little later than the average coed and earned a B.A. in English, then she dove off the deep end into a full-time writing career—a wish come true.

Susan enjoys writing about people who take a chance on love, sometimes against all odds. She loves warm, strong heroes and good-hearted, self-reliant heroines, and will always believe in happily ever after.

More can be learned about her at www.susancrosby.com.

For Steve—
brother, friend and cohort in childhood adventures.
Thanks for all the times you got me out of trouble—
and into it.

Chapter One

Denise Watson wondered if Gideon Falcon would be on time for his three o'clock appointment. She was an if-I'm-not-five-minutes-early-I'm-late kind of person herself, but he didn't come across as a man who kept a close eye on the clock.

Anticipating his arrival, she stood at a window of her corner office, overlooking a bustling downtown Sacramento intersection. She'd moved her domestic-and-clerical-help agency, At Your Service, to this prestigious location a year ago, after four years of growing the business. She loved the view of the city skyline from her window.

From three stories up, Denise spotted a motorcycle zip into a just-vacated space on the street below. It had to be Gideon. A motorcycle would suit him—he was in the business of adventure, after all, flying planes and helicopters into remote areas, guiding office-bound executives on treks into the wilderness. He wouldn't use conventional transportation, not even in mid-December, with rain predicted by commute time.

She watched him unhook something long and narrow from the back of his bike, take off his helmet then stride toward her building.

Giving her hair a quick toss over her shoulders, Denise returned to her desk, surprised to hear her pulse pounding in her ears. She'd been more than a little attracted to Gideon that night a month ago at his brother David's wedding, had danced with him for hours, neither of them taking another partner.

What woman wouldn't be attracted? He was breathtakingly handsome, his hair a rich, dark brown, his eyes not just blue, but intense, see-into-your-soul blue. And his body… He had a *body*, all right. He was also about as opposite from her as anyone could be. A daredevil man and a cautious woman mixed about as well as the proverbial oil and water.

Then there was also the minor point that he hadn't called her since.

Her receptionist buzzed her. It was exactly three o'clock. Denise walked out to the reception area to welcome him.

You cut your hair.

It was the first thing that popped into her head when she saw him. It hadn't been superlong before, but long enough to curl down his neck some. Long enough to fall into his face when she'd taken off her heels and he'd leaned closer while they danced. Now he looked like…well, a businessman, although an edgy, rather dangerous one.

"Thank you for fitting me into your schedule," Gideon said as they shook hands, his eyes sparkling as if he knew all the secrets of the universe—or at least the one about whether or not she found him tempting. He wore boots, blue jeans, a white dress shirt and black leather jacket, somehow making casual look chic, as much a dressed-for-success look for his line of work as her outfit was for hers.

"I had a cancellation," she said. They walked toward her office. "It's our busiest time of year, since lots of people need temporary help right before and after Christmas."

"This is my least busy time."

He said it easily, as if it didn't bother him. Maybe he liked the down time, which would drive her crazy. Working satisfied her. "Can I take your jacket?" she asked.

"Thanks." He leaned a cardboard tube against her desk and slipped off the jacket. She was tempted to wrap herself up in it and savor his body heat before hanging it up.

Why didn't you call? The question she wanted to ask most was the one she couldn't ask, even as she felt him checking her out as she moved to sit behind her desk. "How can I help you?" she asked.

"I need a wife."

Disappointment landed on her. Ever since he'd made the appointment, she'd been hoping it was just a ploy to see her again. But it was only business, after all. She hadn't been on his mind as he'd been on hers.

"A wife. Okay," she said, all business now. She pulled her keyboard in front of her and brought up a Request-for-Domestic form. "What kind of skills are you looking for?"

"Wifely skills."

She smiled slightly at that. "Can you be a little more specific? Our domestics do everything from errands to party prep to cleaning to child care."

"I don't need someone with any of those skills, actually. I need someone to be my wife."

She took her fingers off the keyboard. "I think you have me confused with a matchmaking service."

"You did a good job for my brothers."

He really did want a wife? "Not intentionally."

He slouched in his chair a little, crossed an ankle over a knee. "David called you uncanny, the way you match up employers and employees. You even found Noah a teacher. Not a typical staffing placement for your company, right?"

"That was pure luck. Tricia just happened to come along, and she was qualified. She wasn't even looking for a teaching job."

"And now she and Noah are getting married, and David has already tied the knot," Gideon said easily. "Don't people call your company Wives for Hire?"

"That is the unfortunate nickname that some people use, yes, because our employees assume many of the roles that a wife would."

"Except they can't have sex with the employer."

Denise's pulse fluttered. "There's that, of course, but being a wife certainly entails more than what my company provides, regardless of the sex issue."

"But in my case, what I need is a wife." He paused. "Without the sex."

"You mean a pretend wife?"

"Exactly."

"Why?"

"To help me woo an investor to a project of mine."

His logic intrigued and confused her. "You have to be married to accomplish that?"

"For purely business reasons, yes."

"Well, this is a first. Would you like to hire two-point-five children, too?"

He grinned. "Not necessary. Although a little pregnancy padding could be helpful." He straightened, getting down to details. "Look, I need someone who is intelligent, articulate and isn't intimidated by men who are used to being in charge. Someone who can hold her own, whether it's business or social. I need a woman who brings presence—and stability—to the table."

"I see. And how much are you willing to pay for this paragon?" she asked.

"How much would you charge?"

"I don't have a rate set up for what you need. We'll have to talk to the employee and decide together."

"I don't think you understand, Denise. You're the one I want."

Her body reacted to the bold statement. It took her a moment to recover. "I'm not for hire."

"Why not?"

"I own this company. I run this company. It's more than a full-time job already."

"I could work around your schedule. Weekends and evenings would be okay."

"This is impossible, Gideon."

"No, it isn't. Have dinner with me. We'll talk about it. I brought the plans to show you."

"You think you can butter me up over dinner?"

His smile was wide. "I can try."

"No one would believe we got married," she said. "We hardly know each other."

"Sure they would. We'll tell them how we met at David's bachelor party and how the instant attraction caught us off guard. How we avoided each other for the whole week until the wedding, because neither of us had ever felt like that before, and we weren't sure we could trust it."

His eyes went tender and his voice soft as he continued with the mesmerizing words. "Then at the wedding we danced and talked for hours, our eyes meeting, hands touching, bodies brushing, and we knew, we just knew it was right. *We* were right. That there *is* such a thing as love at first sight, that we decided we didn't want to live without each other for one more sunrise. So we drove to Reno and got married, trying to talk each other out of it the whole drive, but only talking ourselves further into it. It'll be a love story for the ages. Even the most cynical men will believe it, because we'll say it with passion in our eyes. We'll be envied by all."

It took Denise a few seconds to focus again. She'd gotten totally caught up in his fairy tale. Heck, he'd convinced *her*, so she supposed others would believe it, too. Really, who would've thought he was a romantic? She'd figured him for the kind of hero Hemingway wrote about. A survivor. The man you hope is with you when your plane goes down.

Still… "I really don't see how we could pull this off, Gideon. Why would you have kept it a secret from your family for a month?"

"There's no reason for them to ever find out. Most

people will never know, only the ones I'm trying to convince to invest in my project, and I'll bet they don't ask. But just in case, we've got a story. At least take a look at what I'm doing. If I can't convince you of the merits of the project, we'll skip the whole thing. Have dinner with me," he repeated.

She wasn't going to take the job, but she could have dinner with him, as a courtesy to him as David and Noah's brother, anyway, and a potential client. She could better match him with someone from her staffing pool that way, too.

She linked her fingers and set them on the desktop, all business. "You'll have to wait or come back. I've got appointments at four and four-thirty." She didn't get to see his reaction, because he stood and grabbed his jacket off the hook, keeping his back to her.

"I'll be here at five, if that works for you," he said. He picked up the tube and passed it to her. "Can I leave this with you for now?"

"Sure." She walked him out. "Maybe I should just order Chinese here? We could use my conference room."

He put a hand on her elbow, stopping her, then looked into her eyes, into her soul, in that way he had. "Let me take you out, Denise. Please."

You couldn't have asked me out a month ago? "All right."

He slid his hand up to her shoulder and squeezed. The simple gesture kick-started her hormones again. Was her face as red as it felt? Could he tell what he was doing to her?

"See you at five," he said.

She nodded, then walked back to her office window and waited until he emerged from the building. Instead of getting on his motorcycle he headed toward the Capitol Mall nearby. He didn't strike her as much of a shopper, but then it was almost Christmas, and he did have nieces and nephews.

"Hel-*lo?*"

Denise snapped to attention at the sound of her assistant's voice right next to her. "What, Stacy?"

"I said he's cute." She gestured out the window. "Your Mr. Falcon. I assume he's David and Noah's brother."

"Yes. The middle brother."

"Is he looking to hire someone, too? Wouldn't it be funny if he also found the love of his life like his brothers did?"

"I would say that's a long shot."

Stacy shrugged, her short black hair bouncing a little. At twenty-eight, she was a year younger than Denise, six inches shorter, and a size two to Denise's size twelve. Stacy had been Denise's first hire when she'd started the business, and was being groomed to take over when Denise went ahead with her expansion/franchise plans. They'd also become good friends.

"What's he looking for?" Stacy asked.

"Me."

"You? Oh, I see. It's not business. It's personal."

Was it personal? Didn't he know anyone else who could play the role of his wife? "We met at the wedding," Denise said, not knowing whether it truly was business or personal. Maybe both?

"You could do worse," Stacy said.

"And have."

Stacy laughed. "So, are you going out with him?"

"Yes, for dinner tonight."

"I'll bet he's a good kisser." She sighed.

Denise hadn't gotten the chance to find out, even though he'd had opportunities at the wedding, especially when he'd walked her to her car at the end of the night. There was something about him that said he knew how to please, that he gave every experience his all. She'd felt it a month ago, and had been staggered by it again now.

"Let me know," Stacy said over her shoulder as she left the office.

"You'll be the first," Denise answered, but she knew it was a lie.

She'd learned her lesson. This time she wouldn't kiss and tell.

In a quiet restaurant a block from her office, Gideon sipped a beer as he waited for Denise to finish reading his business plan. He admired her all-black, all-business outfit of silk blouse, slim skirt and three-inch heels, which brought her almost eye-to-eye with him. She was exactly as he remembered—and had been trying to forget—five feet eight inches of perfect proportions, deep green eyes that were too serious most of the time and hair a shiny brown that flowed over her shoulders....

Hair whose roots told another story. A blond story. He'd been wondering for a month why she dyed her blond hair brown. Hiding something? If so, what?

Their server brought their salads. Denise set aside the papers. "So," she said. "You're trying to buy a cross-country ski resort."

"The Trails. It's on the Nevada side of Lake Tahoe."
He stabbed a tomato and gave his spiel. "It has hugely
underutilized potential, as you can see. Except for
during the snow months, it's being used as grazing land.
The owners, Ed and Joanne Baker, built fifteen cabins
on the property in the mid-sixties. I want to tear down
everything and start new, create a year-round recreation
site—cross-country skiing still, but also hiking and
mountain-bike trails, horseback riding, even wilderness
packing and camping, guided trips. And then there
would be the accommodations. A spa, of course. Can't
not have one these days. Maybe a conference or retreat
area. Plus a great restaurant and hotel."

Something flickered in her eyes, but she looked at
her salad so fast he couldn't read it.

"How much time do you have?" she asked.

"I have to present my offer to the Bakers in ten
days. As you can see, I've got everything lined up
except complete financial backing. I've been scram-
bling for a couple of months since Max Beauregard
died. He was going to partner with me on it. I would
buy the land and build the trails. He would build the
hotel. Did you know Max?"

"I didn't know him personally, but he was pretty
young when he died, wasn't he?"

"Thirty-seven. Made a killing in the tech business
early on. He was one of my first clients when I started my
business, then he spread the word to his friends and as-
sociates. Plus he gave me great financial advice through
the years. Incredible advice that changed my life."

"So, what happened? Did he die before you signed
contracts?"

"No, it was a done deal. His widow, Ann, can't follow through."

"Isn't she legally bound?"

"Yes—except for a particular requirement the Bakers have. They will only sell to a young married couple who will keep The Trails name and family-friendly environment. The Beauregards qualified us for that requirement, even though the project was really mine. With them out of the picture, I tried to find another couple, but I need a couple with a whole lot of money who are also interested in this project. They don't grow on trees. Ann gave me some leads that didn't pan out. Then last month she said it was too bad I wasn't married, because I was the one with the interest, after all. Then all I had to do was find a backer for the hotel. Not an easy thing, either, but easier."

"Why couldn't she still be your investor?"

"It was Max's project, really. And I don't feel like forcing her to adhere to the contract when she doesn't have a love for it."

"I certainly understand that. But the Bakers' requirement sure seems odd to me." Denise gestured with her fork. "A supposedly happily married couple could make the deal and get divorced a week later. How could the Bakers enforce that?"

"Technically, they can't."

"So you plan to be *married* until the deal is done, then end it? Not exactly a fine example of character."

"Where is it written that only married men have good character? I want The Trails. I know what I can do with it. And what qualifies me is my personal need and expectation not only to provide a family-friendly environment, but one with a bigger scope, one that keeps up with ever-changing interests, to challenge families to play together, to be active together. They're not lofty goals. They're possible. If I have to pretend that I'm married in order to prove what I can do, then that's what I'll do."

"What if they find out you aren't?"

"How could they? Only you and I would know the truth. If we don't tell anyone else, how could they possibly find out?"

She broke off a piece of roll, buttered it but didn't take a bite as she mulled over his words. "Okay, I get it. How many investors do you think it's going to take?"

"One."

"Seriously?"

"I don't want more than one, someone who's got pockets deep enough not to need returns for several years. I could never please or pay off a group of investors. At best I could only get myself a small percentage by putting the deal together and working it. That's not what I want, not what I've worked for, saved for."

"You're looking for a fifty-fifty relationship?"

"In an ideal world, I'd do fifty-one/forty-nine so that I could always have the final say. The chances of getting someone to agree to it are slim."

She set her fork on her empty plate and took a sip of her wine. He could see the wheels turning in her head.

She lifted her glass to him. "Well, the project looks incredible to me. For the most part."

He smiled at that. "For the most part?"

She shrugged. "I'm concerned about the hotel."

Something in her tone intrigued him. "Max and I

hired James Madigan. He's an architect who specializes in hotels."

"Yes, I know who he is."

The way she said it implied not only that she knew him, but she didn't approve. "You object to his plan?"

"Since you asked, yes. Don't get me wrong. He's great at doing hotel chains—you know, keeping with a tradition already established—but he's not good at fresh design. This plan he did for you is okay, but it needs to be more rustic, more suited to the environment. And the interior design is…well, it's like a lot of other resort hotels. There aren't any surprises."

"Should there be?" He found himself unexpectedly turned on by the focused businesswoman. He generally liked women who were daring and adventurous, like him. Bold. Had even married one—not that it had worked out. He'd figured Denise for being time-and-detail oriented, without much give, but packaged in a supersexy body that he hadn't stopped thinking about— the primary reason he'd kept his distance this month. He hadn't needed distractions. But then he couldn't get her out of his head—

"*I* certainly like being surprised when I travel," she said. "I imagine the views at this resort are spectacular, given the location in the Sierras. They need to be taken advantage of better." She tapped the stack of paperwork. "The guest rooms are doing that fairly well, but the common rooms aren't. Not fully. If I—"

She stopped herself, smiled apologetically. "Sorry. I didn't mean to take over."

He considered her in a new light. He'd known she was intelligent, but he hadn't seen fire in her eyes, not like this. "There's no time to change the plans," he said. "Ten days…"

"Yes, there is. It doesn't have to be perfect, just the core idea with a reasonable estimate of costs, right?"

"True." Their server took away their salad plates, replacing them with their entrées—salmon for her, rib-eye steak for him. "But we're talking an immediate turnaround. If I don't have a plan to show, I can't interest anyone in the project."

"It can be done."

"How?"

She didn't answer right away. After a long, increasingly tense moment, she said, "You don't know who I am, do you? I thought maybe you'd come to me with this proposition because you knew, but you don't."

He focused on her, confused. A month ago he'd spent a whole evening staring into her face, holding her close. She was beautiful, but not recognizable beyond the time they'd spent together. "Should I?"

"If I tell you that most of my life people called me Deni?"

It took a few seconds to make the connection. Deni Watson. He could even picture her—the way she used to be. Blond hair, worn short and wild. A size zero, or two or four. He didn't know how to measure such things. Best friends with Dani something or other. *Deni and Dani*, their names always linked in the tabloid headlines. Daughter of Lionel Watson, hotel magnate, owner of the luxurious Watson Hotels chain founded by his late father years ago.

Deni Watson, young, headstrong and beautiful. And bad girl extraordinaire.

Chapter Two

Denise knew the moment he registered who she was. She continued to eat her salmon, even as his gaze never wavered except to probe deeper.

"I guess you *do* know hotels," he said. "I don't pay much attention to the gossip magazines, but I do recall a lot of speculation when you disappeared from the scene. How long ago was that?"

"Five years." She lifted her glass of chardonnay in a toast to creative journalists everywhere. "Apparently I either had a disfiguring car accident or a prince's secret baby."

"Or a very long stint in rehab," he said.

"That was my personal favorite. I certainly partied now and then, but I didn't make a fool of myself, except once. A moment that haunted me for years."

"Why did you go into hiding?" he asked. "I'm

assuming that's what you did, anyway, since you changed your hair color and put on some weight."

"Some?" She'd gained more than twenty-five pounds.

"Enough to put you at a healthy weight now," he said, studying her. "And you're right. Most people probably wouldn't recognize you."

"Interest in me may have faded, but I still pop up in where-are-they-now articles and video segments. But you asked why I left my old life. The short answer is that I had something to prove, and I needed to do it without the power of my father's name behind my success."

"To prove to *him*?"

"Mostly to myself." She set down her wineglass. "I'm telling you this because while you may think I would be an asset to your cause, in truth, I could just as easily be a liability, depending on how someone feels about me. And, believe me, people generally have strong opinions about it. So you may want to rethink your plan. I'm sure I could come up with someone to fill the part for you."

She didn't want to come up with someone else for him, she realized, had changed her mind when she studied his plan. His project intrigued and excited her.

So did he, in an even bigger way. She'd be taking on a big risk personally because he, too, intrigued and excited her, unlike anyone else had for a long time.

"Are you saying you'll do it?" he asked. He'd gone still and serious.

She'd fallen in love with the idea of his resort, but she couldn't let him see the extent of her interest yet. She needed to be sensible first. She didn't want to lose her credibility—or have her heart broken. "I'd like to take the plans home and study them further before I decide. I'd also like to see the scale model you talk about in your plans. And I'd like to see the site in person."

He half smiled. "It's not like I'm asking you for money."

"I can't lend my name if I don't fully support what you're doing. And we have to go into this assuming that some people will figure out who I am. I don't flaunt it, but I don't hide it either."

"I respect that." Their server picked up their plates, offered dessert menus, then left when they declined. "Are you free tomorrow?" he asked.

They worked out a plan for the next day as they left the restaurant, stopping outside the entrance. She slipped into her raincoat as he held it, then she pulled her mini-umbrella from her briefcase.

"Not gonna rain," he said, looking up. "Not for a couple of hours, anyway."

"I suppose you can smell it in the air or something, mountain man."

He smiled. "The point is, I *can't* smell it."

"I'll bet you're very good at your job."

His shrug could mean anything.

"Where's your car?" he asked.

"I walked. I usually do." She pointed ahead. "That's my building."

"I'd offer you a ride on Hilda, but I don't have another helmet with me. And you'd have to hike up your skirt…." He angled toward her, looked about to say something, then stopped himself. "I'll walk you home."

She wished he'd said whatever had been on the tip of his tongue. "That's not necessary, Gideon, but thanks. You should get going before the rain does come, just in case your nose isn't right," she added, even though she figured he knew what he was talking about. "You've got about an hour's drive, I think?"

"Are you always this bossy?" He softened the words with a grin. "I want to see you safely home. Be gracious."

"Who's the bossy one?" She wasn't afraid to walk home alone, even though the hustle and bustle of commute time had passed. There wasn't the usual crowd to get lost in.

He rested his hand at the small of her back to get her moving. Every hormone, every nerve ending in her body reacted.

"You always walk in those stilts?" he asked.

"I left my walking shoes in the office." Her ego had overruled her usual sensibilities. She'd caught Gideon admiring her legs in the high heels.

"Hilda's your motorcycle, I gather," she said, needing to make conversation, needing to do anything to slow the arousal racing through her, clamoring for attention.

"Yep."

"Why Hilda?"

"It means ready for battle. Hilda Harley is her whole name. She's a full pedigree. So, should I call you Denise or Deni?"

"Probably Denise, if you don't want people to guess who I am. They sound like completely different names, don't you think? Denise is pretty old-fashioned sounding."

"I don't know. I'm thinking it might be helpful for people to know who you are."

She frowned at him. "You must not remember the reputation I had."

"Was it deserved?"

"Not to the degree it was put out there."

"People have an impression of who I am, too," he said, "based on the work I do, as if I wouldn't be responsible or reliable. I'm responsible for life and limb while my clients are with me. I take that seriously."

"So then, that's even more reason to keep my identity a secret. If they got the impression they were working with two flighty people, there'd be no chance of success." She was aware of him beside her. Aware of his height, his ability to stay focused, his muscular frame, his strong hands. David's wife had told her about him. How David and Noah went to Gideon for advice, that nothing seemed to faze him. How the brothers all had different mothers but were raised together, their father getting sole custody of each of them. There was a story there, something to ask another time, when they knew each other better.

"You're quiet," he said as they waited at a signal.

"You've given me a lot to think about."

"Good."

They crossed the street, were only a block from her high-rise condo complex. "What happens if you don't get the backing, Gideon?"

"I keep doing what I've been doing for all these years. Maybe I'll find another location and try again. I don't think in negative terms. I believe this is going to work, one way or another. And I like challenges."

"Why don't you go ahead and buy the land, since you have the money for it, then take the time to get a partner?"

"Because if I can't build the rest of it to create the whole package, I would never have enough of a business to do more than the Bakers have—which pays the bills, but that's all. I can't commit to it without knowing there's a payoff for me."

"And seeming to be married, even though it's a lie, is critical to your success."

"Without question."

"But no pressure, right?" she asked with a smile.

"Of course not."

They reached her building. "Would you like to come up?" The invitation came spontaneously, not a conscious decision but an emotional one. If she'd taken a moment to think about it—

"Thanks. I think I should hit the road. Beat the rain." He looked up. "What floor are you on?"

She was glad he'd turned her down, wasn't ready for him to be in her space. "Lucky thirteen. The view's amazing. Plus there's underground parking, a swimming pool, a library and a fitness room. The amenities are great."

"I have all that, too. You'll see tomorrow." He passed her the tube with the plans rolled up inside.

"I'll be at your place by nine," she said.

"Come hungry. I'll fix you breakfast."

He cooks, too? "Okay."

"In the meantime…" He dug into his jacket pocket, pulled out a jeweler's box and opened it. Inside was a platinum-and-three-diamonds wedding band. "You'll need to wear this tomorrow."

The ring was stunning. Her first instinct was to try it on. She curled her hands into fists instead. "Pretty sure of yourself, Gideon."

He shrugged slightly. "I knew if you were any kind of businesswoman you'd want to see the site in person. You would be there as my wife."

"I haven't given you my answer yet. What if you show up with a different 'wife' later?"

"You've decided."

His confidence irked her—and pleased her. She liked that he had that much sense of himself.

He plucked the ring from the box and held it up. "Want to see if it fits?"

She held out her hand. The ring seemed on fire, as if chiding her for telling a lie by pretending to be married. "It's fine," she said, then tugged it off immediately and handed it back to him. "Did you get one for yourself?"

"I did. It's plain." Instead of tucking the ring back in the box, he pulled out a tissue-wrapped packet that contained a long silver chain. He slipped her ring onto it, lifted it over her head and let it dip inside her blouse.

She felt it slide into her cleavage, then nestle.

"For when you're not playing the part," he said.

Her mind went blank as he turned her around.

"Thank you for doing this," he said, and then he kissed her, a soft, electric brush of his lips against hers. "See why I can't come up?"

"It takes two to tango."

"Yes, and we've both got the moves." He gave her a knowing look. "I'll see you in the morning, Mrs. Falcon."

She laughed but made no move to go into the

building. She didn't want the evening to end. She couldn't remember the last time she'd felt that way, and this hadn't even been a date.

Well… actually, it had been considerably more than a date. She'd just sort of gotten married.

"I can't leave until you're safely indoors," he said, interrupting her thoughts.

It would be useless to tell him she came and went from this building every day without incident, so she went inside. He lifted a hand to her, then took off, his stride long and easy. She watched until he was out of sight. In her condo a few minutes later she stared at her phone. She'd almost asked him to call when he got home so that she knew he made it okay, before the rain. He would've laughed at her.

So instead she waited a little over an hour, then dialed his number.

He picked up on the first ring. "Safe and sound. And dry," he said instead of hello.

She hesitated. She really needed to remember how intuitive he was, that he would've seen in her eyes that she was worried about him riding Hilda in the rain. "That's not why I called."

"You have some burning question that can't wait until morning?"

She heard laughter in his voice. Lighten up, she told herself. Have fun, like he is.

"It doesn't bother me that you were worried," he said before she could think up a reason for calling. "It's nice. Wifely." He did laugh then, soft and low. "Did you try on the ring again?"

Her face heated. She'd not only tried it on, it was still

on. Really, how could she work with someone who'd figured her out so well, so soon?

"I gather you don't want to lie to me, so you're keeping silent instead," he said.

"Or it could be that your ego doesn't need more feeding."

"Touché. We're going to need to talk about this attraction, don't you think? Get it out in the open so that we can work together?"

"I think that's a good idea, Gideon." She hadn't figured him to be the kind of man to "talk." She'd spent her life around men who didn't talk about anything risky, emotional or otherwise.

"It'll make great breakfast conversation. Anything you hate or are allergic to?"

"I'm game for anything."

"Anything?"

"Food-wise," she said with a smile. He was going to keep her on her toes.

"See you tomorrow morning, Mrs. Falcon."

She tried to think of something witty to say in return, but came up empty. "Good night, mountain man." She hung up, left her hand curved over the receiver. She stared at the brilliant wedding band.

She couldn't fault the man for his taste, or his brains. Or his body. He was the real deal, the whole package.

And if she wasn't careful, he would end up being the death of her grand plans for herself.

Chapter Three

Denise thoroughly enjoyed her drive the next morning up into the gorgeous and green Sierra foothills. The farther away she got from Sacramento, the more her shoulders relaxed, which surprised her. She loved her city life. She had a prosperous business, good friends and a busy social life. She thrived on action and purpose. This trip was making her forget work completely.

Except, of course, there was something else to worry about—Gideon. She'd taken some risks in her life, but this was one of the riskiest, getting involved with a man embarking on a new enterprise that would take years of focus and concentration.

At five minutes to nine, she turned into Gideon's driveway and followed it a long way back, not seeing the house until she'd made a couple turns. She had to laugh. He'd said his house had all the amenities of her condo, including underground parking. She guessed he'd meant the parking area under his deck, which stood probably twelve feet above the ground, the front of the house raised on thick beams. A silver-gray SUV was parked below the deck, Hilda next to it.

The structure itself, more cabin than house, melded aesthetically with the surroundings of oak and pine trees, evergreen shrubs and craggy rocks. Frost rimed shady spots.

She parked in a graded space off to the side. By the time she'd gotten out of her car, he was walking toward her. The quiet struck her—even the fact she couldn't hear his footsteps. She shivered, wondering what the temperature was.

"Welcome," he said, his breath billowing in the cold air, his gaze intense.

She wanted to hug him hello. Instead she said, "This is breathtaking, Gideon. I'm looking for the swimming pool, however."

"You can see it best from the back porch, upstairs."

"Lead the way. I can't wait to see your library and fitness center, too."

He grinned. "They may not match up with your own on-site amenities, but then I value privacy more than size." He headed up the path that led to steps hewn of heavy timber. They crossed his front deck, where comfortable cushioned chairs and wooden side tables made the perfect place to sit and think, to enjoy the birds and squirrels in the branches above, or whatever other wildlife passed through the property. Deer, she supposed. Foxes.

Tall, thick trees blocked the wind, filtered the sun and

scented the air with pine, a reminder, too, that Christmas was coming.

The cabin's exterior was built of logs. She couldn't guess how old it was, but it looked well maintained.

"The swimming pool," he announced gesturing toward a small, sapphire-blue lake a couple hundred yards in the distance. Smoke rose from chimneys here and there in the landscape between his place and the lake.

"You swim laps, I suppose," she said.

"Daily."

"I'll bet." She rested her hands on the railing and took it all in. "It's stunning. So is your cabin."

"Thanks. I built it myself."

She wondered why she wasn't surprised. "That must be satisfying."

"Beyond measure." He eyed his house, looking pleased.

"You're a man of many talents, aren't you? Very of-the-earth." Very macho, she wanted to add. She was more used to executives—the kind of men Gideon probably took on adventure treks into the wilderness. Men more like his brothers, actually.

"You're wearing the ring," he said, putting his hand over hers, rubbing the stones with his thumb. "I'm going to take that to mean you've decided to be my wife."

Heat snaked through her. "Your pretend wife. You're wearing yours, as well."

He nodded, a smile lurking at the corners of his mouth, drawing her gaze to the lips that had kissed her lightly last night, leaving a desire for more.

"There are details to work out," she said.

"Like?"

"Legalities."

"Salary," he stated.

She turned around and crossed her arms, leaning against the wood at her waist. "I don't want us to have a contract through my business, but something personal."

"I'm willing to deal. What are you looking for?"

"No salary."

His brows went up. "Why not?"

"I know your intention was to hire me as a kind of figurehead, someone to show off, but I can be of much more help than that. I have contacts, you know."

He hesitated. "Let's talk about it over breakfast." He led the way into his house, the front of which was almost entirely glass, allowing an incredible view from inside.

She smelled bacon, her all-time favorite food, although she wouldn't have admitted that to anyone. Logs crackled in a big, stone fireplace. The large, open floor plan included the kitchen, living room and dining room, its table set with very masculine black-and-brown dishes and placemats. A carved wooden bowl heaped with pinecones made up the centerpiece.

He'd already moved into the kitchen. She ambled over to the counter and eased onto a stool to watch him work.

He pointed to several bowls on the counter, filled with fresh ingredients—tomatoes, shredded cheese, sautéed mushrooms and green onions. "I'm making omelets. What's your pleasure?"

"The works, thanks."

"And salsa?"

"Perfect."

He grabbed a piece of crisp bacon kept warm in an aluminum foil packet and passed it to her. His eyes were smiling, as if he knew, absolutely knew for a fact she was dying for a piece. "Coffee?" he asked.

"Love some. But I can get it."

"You're my guest. Relax." He poured her a cup, added one sugar and a smidgen of cream, then set the mug in front of her. When she looked at him in surprise, he said, "I'm assuming your tastes haven't changed since the wedding reception."

He turned back to the stove, added butter to a hot pan and started fixing an omelet like a seasoned chef. She nibbled on bacon, sipped her coffee and enjoyed the show, which seemed effortless and efficient. He turned the omelet onto a plate, then quickly assembled another exactly the same. He poured warmed-up salsa over the top of each, added bacon and sourdough toast to each plate, then carried them to the table.

"You're fun to watch," she said, taking her seat. "Have you worked as a chef?"

"Sort of. I cook for my clients, but I generally use a small camp stove or an open fire pit for that. And I've always liked to cook. I learned very young because Noah, being the oldest, was given way too many chores as we were growing up, and he hated cooking, so I took over. I'm the grill master in our family."

They ate in silence for a couple of minutes.

"You're good," she said, toasting him with a forkful of eggs.

"Do you like to cook?"

"Yes." She looked around his living space then realized there were no photos out, no family in view.

There were none in her place, either, except in her bedroom. "How close are you to your brothers' homes?"

"About fifteen minutes."

"I went to both houses to pick up Tricia and Valerie for Valerie's bachelorette party. They have beautiful homes."

She looked at him over the rim of her mug. "I heard that all three of you were equal partners after your father died."

"True. I sold my share to them after a year or so. The job required heavy-duty sales. I was good at it, but I hated it. Falcon Motorcars has done just fine without me. David and Noah have also done just fine without me on board, too. They took what our father started and made it a success many times over what he'd done with it. I expect this deal will do the same for me."

"You'll be a millionaire."

He smiled slightly. "That wouldn't be something new for me. I took my profits from the family business and made smart investments, thanks initially to Max Beauregard's advice."

She'd already figured out he was incredibly bright. "How long ago did you build your house?"

"Two years. After my divorce." He stood and took their plates to the kitchen, then ran water over them in the sink.

She didn't ask if she could help, just pitched in, and he didn't refuse.

"Sore subject?" she asked.

"What? The divorce? No. It laid me low at the time, but after the fact I realized I'd married her for the wrong reasons. She admitted the same. At least I'd been smart enough to protect my inheritance with a prenup. I've always lived on what I made. When I was first on my own, I got myself into a couple of ventures that were disastrous. I even got Noah and David involved. They said they weren't going to risk it anymore. It forced me to figure out what to do. And as soon as I got my adventure business running, it paid off. Marriage seemed like the next logical step."

Denise appreciated his openness, particularly admitting to his failures. She never liked anyone to know about hers.

She found dish soap and started filling the sink with hot water, not seeing a dishwasher anywhere. "No children?"

"No." He reached around her to drop some dishes into the filling sink, his chest brushing her back, triggering little explosions all through her.

She liked the sensation, way too much. If they were going to work together she should avoid contact with him now that she knew how much and how easily he affected her, but she hadn't felt like this for a long time, if ever. She didn't mind experimenting to see how far they could go.

She just needed to keep her heart intact, her life on schedule.

"When did you tell the Bakers you're married?" she asked.

"A month ago."

"What have you told them about me?"

"That you're beautiful and brilliant. Obviously, I was psychic," he said, smiling. "I don't remember everything I said, exactly. Joanne asked a lot of questions. That woman believes more in marriage than anyone I've met."

"Do we want children?" she asked.

He grabbed a dishtowel and a rinsed plate, his hip resting against the countertop. "Absolutely. As soon as possible. I'm thirty-two, after all, and you're—I don't even know."

"Twenty-nine." She wondered if what he'd told the Bakers was the truth or a story. "So, I'm not on the pill, after all?"

He met her gaze directly. "No pill. No condoms. Nothing."

"Hmm. Am I giving up my business in Sacramento? Did you tell them your wife works?"

"I'm pretty sure I avoided the topic. As for our story today, we should probably say we haven't decided yet. That you may get someone to run it."

"Which means I'm scrapping my plans to open At Your Service franchises around the country, I guess."

He whistled. "Is that your goal? You don't think small."

"Nope." She wanted to create her own empire.

"Have you given yourself a time frame?" Gideon asked.

"I have a schedule."

"Of course you do."

She smiled. "San Francisco next year."

"Will you move there?"

"Temporarily. It's a good place for me to branch out, because I've already made inroads there. Los Angeles after that, probably." She rinsed the last pan and passed it to Gideon, then wiped down the counter as he finished putting things away.

"And the real Gideon? Do you want children?"

"Definitely. I need a few years' cushion to get the business going. How about you?"

"Also definitely. Just not yet. Not in the schedule."

"Exactly. Mine, either."

"So. I'd like to see your scale model," she said, deciding to change the subject, which had gotten too personal.

"It's in my office."

They walked past a large bathroom on the left and an even larger bedroom on the right. She caught a glimpse of masculine decor, including a huge pine bed covered with a green-and-black quilt. At the back of the house was a room that stretched across the whole width. An office took up one side, exercise equipment the other. One wall was bookcases, filled top to bottom. The view through the large windows went on forever, the lake a shimmering gem, the forest beyond thick and luxuriant.

"Welcome to my library and gym," he said, his eyes sparkling. "All the necessary amenities."

"So I see. I'm surprised you don't have a dog. You seem like a dog person."

"I'm gone too much. It's in my plans, though."

"A teacup poodle, I suppose."

"Fifi. You got me all figured out."

She wandered to a large table on which sat his scale model. She took her time studying it. He waited silently, letting her review it on her own. "You built this model, too?" she asked.

"Yep."

"How long have you been working on the project?"

"A year on this site specifically. It took some time to get environmental impact studies done and to analyze the economics of other sites similar to this. I've seen plenty of family resorts around the country and a few in Europe. I took the best of what I saw, then created what I consider is the perfect environment. But technically I've been studying this business for nine years. I believe I know what will work and what won't. Except that I'm not an expert in hotel design like you, obviously," he added.

"I don't know that I'm an expert, either, but I know what I like, what I've always thought I would build if I had the chance. I got my bachelor's degree in hotel management, but I started working in the Watson Hotels Los Angeles when I was fourteen. I was like a sponge."

"Why aren't you working for your father?"

"Long story." She turned back to the model and traced a trail with her finger from top to bottom.

"Sore subject?" he asked, putting a hand on her back.

She wanted to turn into him and lay her head on his shoulder. Be held. Even after seven years the wound was raw. "Yeah. But dead and buried."

"I don't think so. Looks like we both have father issues. Do you see your dad?"

"We're not estranged, but we're not close." She'd dogged his footsteps her whole childhood, adoring him, putting him on a sky-high pedestal, then he'd crushed her. Denise took a few steps away from the temptation of confiding in and accepting comfort from Gideon. "I'm ready to see the site in person, if you are. We can talk business as we go."

"There's an issue we need to address before we head out," he said.

"What's that?"

"The attraction between us."

Just the thought kick-started her heart into a powerful rhythm. "You have ideas?" she asked.

He moved a little closer. "As much as I'd like to say we should ignore it and see if it goes away, I'm more realistic than that. We have to pretend we're married. That alone will require that we look comfortable together, that we seem intimate. It's easy to recognize people who are lovers, because they move into each other's space easily."

His words added fuel to her already burning fire. "Are you suggesting we become lovers as part of this deal?"

His smile was slow and sexy. "I wouldn't turn it down. But no, that's not what I'm saying. I'm saying you shouldn't take a step back when I get close." He moved within touching range.

She stood her ground. "In public."

He didn't speak, but he picked up her left hand and kissed her palm, his thumb pressing into the ring.

"Have you always been a romantic?" she asked.

"Yes." He kept her hand in his.

"You're a rarity."

"Am I?"

"Everyone is so straightforward these days. And self-focused. Dates are more like negotiations."

"You haven't met the right men, I think." He pulled her into his arms and started dancing with her without music. "We fit. That can't be ignored. I noticed it right away."

"You didn't call me this whole month." She hadn't meant to say that, as if she'd been waiting by the phone for his call. She'd actually stopped doing that after two weeks....

"Not because I didn't want to see you, Mrs. Falcon."

She wondered when—or if—she would stop reacting to him calling her that. "That makes no sense."

"This project has consumed me and will continue to if I manage to find a partner. You wouldn't like my lack of attention. It would kill any hope of a relationship."

"You see me as high maintenance?"

He stopped dancing but didn't let her go. "I see you as a beautiful woman who deserves someone's complete attention."

"I'm busy, too. Maybe I would be happy taking what I could get."

He ran his fingers across her lips until she parted them, then he kissed her. "If that's true," he said, brushing his lips back and forth against hers, "you've got the chance now to test your theory."

He settled his mouth on hers, wrapped his arms around her. She couldn't stop a needy moan from escaping, which made him deepen the kiss even more. He slipped his tongue inside her mouth and moved his hands to her waist, sliding up her rib cage, his thumbs resting just under breasts. She moved against him, pressing her hips flush with his, enjoying his powerful body, the feel of his broad hands, the taste and heat of his mouth. She went up on tiptoe, wrapping her arms around his neck, wanting more. Now.

He nipped at her mouth then pulled away. "I'll bet you're very demanding in bed," he said when she finally opened her eyes. He looked as aroused as she, as needy as she.

"Are you up to it?" she asked.

"What do you think?"

"My assistant decided you'd be a good kisser."

"And what's your opinion?"

"That you exceeded expectation." She didn't know why she was being so honest with him. Maybe she shouldn't flatter him, shouldn't let him know how much he turned her on. She'd just slipped into the role of his wife—his adoring wife—as if born to it.

"Same with you." He moved back a little more. "It complicates things. I knew it would."

"Honesty works for me, Gideon. I can handle anything but silence. I hate silence. Tell me the truth, whatever it is. Don't ever make me guess."

"Deal. Shall we get on the road?"

She put a hand on his arm. "Maybe we should talk about what I want out of this arrangement, in case you want to change your mind."

"Okay."

"I want credit," she said. "And a piece of the action if I'm the one to find you a partner."

He stared at her for a good long time. She'd made her decision. Nothing he said would sway her. She could be a part of his success, if he let her. She didn't know how much give he had, or even if he would compromise. He might accept her input on the hotel, but on anything else? She didn't know yet.

"You've got about an hour in the car to convince me," he said, then gestured toward the door. "After you, Mrs. Falcon."

She took that as a hopeful sign.

Chapter Four

Denise counted cars in the parking lot when they pulled into The Trails. Two massive snowstorms had hit the area since Thanksgiving, creating a solid base, making for good cross-country skiing, yet the parking lot was about half full, maybe a hundred cars.

"Is this the usual number for a Saturday?" she asked, unbuckling her seat belt.

"I don't know. The season just started. The last time I was here, the cattle were being trucked out."

"If this is it, I can see why they've only eked out a living all these years. How much do they advertise?"

"Not much. Mostly they depend on repeat customers. The Bakers are good people but not great businesspeople. They wanted to raise their children here, and they needed a business to sustain them enough to do that. I think they would tell you they have no regrets."

"You haven't said if you have competition."

"They've let it be known they're interested in selling, but I don't know specifically if there are others. I would assume so, although it can't be easy finding someone to meet their requirements who can also afford to buy."

"Why the Christmas Eve deadline?"

"I asked that. Ed and Joanne just smiled at each other. I'm assuming it's sentimental."

She eyed him. He was dressed much like he had been when he'd come to her office the day before. She figured he knew a suit and tie wouldn't be helpful dealing with this couple. She'd also dressed appropriately, including snow boots. "You really are a risk taker, even to the point of risking all the capital you've grown and protected all these years."

"Not getting any younger." His grin seemed a little reckless to her, a little dangerous. He was a fascinating combination of the kind of men she'd dated when she was known as Deni and those she dated now, but she found herself drawn more to the edgier side of him. He wouldn't back down from anything that mattered to him. She liked that. A lot.

"Didn't you take chances starting your business?" he asked. "It's an unavoidable part of success. Some people have the nerve for it and some don't."

"I hadn't looked at it that way." She glanced out the windshield and saw a woman climb the steps to a building at the far end of the parking lot. "Are the Bakers expecting us?"

"They're expecting *me*." He pointed ahead. "There's

Mrs. Baker on the porch. Joanne. She's sixty-eight. Ed's a year older. They're both fit and sociable, and look about ten years younger."

"Anything else? I'm sure, as your wife, they would expect me to know more about them than that."

"I can't—Oh, they celebrated their fiftieth anniversary recently. They have two daughters."

Gideon opened his door. "Ready?"

Denise climbed out. She grabbed the paperwork while he brought the scale model. She was nervous, she realized, feeling it in her chest. She'd been exposed to so many unusual situations while growing up that she rarely felt nervous or uncomfortable in any setting. But she didn't want to mess this up for Gideon—or herself. Too much was at stake. For him and for her. She had something to prove, too. She'd successfully built a business, but to also help build a hotel? Yes, she wanted that. Passionately.

"What will happen to your adventure business if you take this on?" she asked.

"I'll run it from here. I already have someone in mind to take charge of it until The Trails is up and running."

They reached the building. Joanne Baker had spotted them and was waiting, smiling. "You have the model! I can't wait to see it. Hello, Gideon," she added with a laugh. "I didn't mean to be rude. I'm just so anxious to see your plans." She stuck out her hand toward Denise. "Hi, I'm Joanne Baker."

"Denise Falcon." Saying it out loud for the first time caught her off-guard. It felt even more strange than hearing Gideon call her Mrs. Falcon, because he always gave it a sexy lilt.

"Well, finally, you brought your wife! I've been dying to meet you," Joanne said. "He's told me so much about you."

He had? Not according to Gideon. Denise gave him a look, and he shrugged.

"I've really been looking forward to meeting you, too," Denise said.

"Oh, look at me. Your hands are full, and I'm gabbing. Come in." Joanne held the door for them. "Ed! Gideon's here. And he's brought a surprise."

The building was multipurpose—ticket booth, ski equipment rental and a small dining room where they sold hot beverages and prepackaged, made-fresh-daily sandwiches. Their conference room was behind the counter and had a window where they could watch for customers. Joanne brought in a carafe of coffee and plate of cookies that looked homemade.

They all examined the model, with Gideon adding more information to fill in the complete picture. Although the Bakers would technically have no say in the final plans, Denise knew that Gideon wanted them to see he would be a good steward of their land.

"Where will you live after you leave here?" Denise asked.

"We're moving to Arizona, of course," Joanne said, frowning as if bothered by the question. "To be near our daughters and our grandchildren."

Yeah, Denise should've known that. What else had Gideon not said?

Ed offered to lead Gideon by snowmobile around the property, to see it in operation, but didn't include Denise. Gideon gave her an apologetic look, then left.

She wanted to handcuff him to a chair so that he could answer the bombardment of questions that would undoubtedly come.

"More coffee?" Joanne asked. "Or maybe you'd like tea instead? I'm sorry I didn't ask that."

"I'm good, thanks. Gideon told me you just celebrated your fiftieth anniversary."

"We went to Hawaii. Our kids and grandkids came, too. That was what made us antsy to get this place sold and move to where it's warm. Our old bones have had enough of the cold." She leaned her elbows on the table. "We were so sorry when Max Beauregard died. We liked him and his wife so much, even though they weren't what we expected as the people who would become the new owners. They were very down to earth, for all that they had so much money you couldn't count it, don't you think?"

"Yes. Very down to earth."

"We thought Gideon would be out of the running after that, but then he surprised us and said he'd gotten married. He hadn't mentioned he was even engaged. How did you meet?"

"We met briefly at a party, then soon after at his brother's wedding."

"Love at first sight?"

Denise smiled at Joanne's girlish tone. "Yes. It caught us both by surprise."

"Did you have a beautiful wedding?"

"We eloped." Denise toyed with her napkin. "We tried to talk ourselves out of it, but really couldn't come up with any good reasons not to do it. Neither of us is impulsive, so we amazed ourselves by going through with it."

"No regrets?"

"None."

"How do you feel about making your home here?"

"It's beautiful." Was that a vague enough answer?

Joanne cocked her head. "Gideon said you were excited about it."

"Who wouldn't be?" *Come back, Gideon. Don't leave me here with her.*

"Are you looking forward to using the trails?"

"I haven't been on skis for years."

"Really? Gideon said you were a fanatic, like him."

"Oh, I am. I am." She was going to kill Gideon. He couldn't have remembered that detail to pass along to her? "I've just been so busy with my job. It'll be wonderful having the course right outside our door."

"Do you think you'll have children soon?"

Finally, something she could answer. "We won't wait too long."

"I imagine not. Especially since you want four."

Denise almost choked. Four? The strikes were piling up against Gideon fast. "Maybe we'll get lucky and have twins," she said. "It runs in the family."

"Well, I've been watching you since got here, both of you. I can see you love each other. It's plain as day."

It is? "He's a wonderful man. The best I've ever met. He'll take good care of your land."

"Yes, both Ed and I feel good about him. And I'm very glad he finally brought you along. We wouldn't have decided without meeting you, too. We couldn't understand why he waited so long to bring you. Almost as if you didn't exist!"

Imagine that. "Have you had other offers?" It wasn't

a question Denise would have asked if Gideon had been there, but she hoped a woman-to-woman talk would yield information he didn't have yet.

"Not yet. Ed and I know we're being overly protective of what we built, but we're both worried that someone will come in here and make a ritzy place out of it. We figure celebrities have enough playgrounds. This has always been a place for families to come. Wholesome and affordable."

"That's Gideon's goal, too," she said quickly. Maybe too quickly, since Joanne's gaze sharpened.

"You know," Joanne said, resting her chin in her hand, "you look familiar."

Denise's mouth went dry. "Do I?" she asked lightly.

"Do you live around here?"

"I live—*lived* in Sacramento."

"You've moved to his cabin in Chance City?"

"At the moment we're splitting our time, at least until a decision is made about The Trails. I have a company in Sacramento. There's lots to work out at the beginning of a relationship, isn't there?" she asked lightly.

"Would I know you from your business?" Joanne asked, obviously not about to give up.

"It's doubtful. I own a temp agency, domestic and clerical help."

The woman shook her head. "We meet with other owners of recreational facilities now and then, but generally in Reno or Tahoe, so I don't think we've run in the same circles. We don't get to Sacramento often." She perked up. "Do you know Jake McCoy? He's from Chance City. He's a regular here, although he hasn't been here yet this season."

She recalled some McCoy brothers being at the bachelorette party and wedding, but not Jake specifically. "I've only just started meeting people from Gideon's town," she said vaguely.

Joanne looked past Denise then. "I've got a customer. Be right back."

"Restroom?" Denise asked.

"Out the door, to the right, then another right," Joanne said as she left.

Denise followed more slowly. She needed to come up with some safe topics to divert the conversation. Her gaze landed on a magazine rack by the door, filled with just about every entertainment magazine and tabloid currently published. So, for all that Joanne Baker was against turning her place into a celebrity haven, she loved to read about them, apparently.

After Joanne returned, Denise tried to lead the conversation, learning in great detail about the woman's children and grandchildren through constant questioning. Finally she needed a break from the constant tension, so she asked to go for a walk, needing to avoid talking, realizing there were really no safe topics. What information Gideon had and hadn't given Joanne, plus Joanne's interest in celebrity gossip, were dangerous for Denise. All of Gideon's plans could be destroyed if she gave a wrong answer, a suspicious answer.

Joanne stayed behind. Denise stuffed her hands in her pockets and headed out, happy for the cold weather to clear her head. She stood in the middle of the parking lot trying to envision the hotel in the setting Gideon had planned.

A vision came to her, a perfect picture of how the

hotel should look, which direction it should face, how deep, how wide, how tall it should be. Built of logs, she decided, like his cabin.

She scrounged in her purse for the pad of paper she always carried and started drawing. She was still standing there when two snowmobiles zipped down the mountain as if racing.

She used her hand to block the sun and focused on the speeding vehicles. Gideon would certainly drive at that speed, but Ed? Her question was answered when they came to a stop at the top of a snowbank near her.

Gideon's face was red from the cold and wind. He shoved up his goggles, and his eyes sparkled. He grinned.

She climbed up the bank and hugged him, enjoying his exuberance, happy to see him, thrilled not to face any more personal questions from Joanne.

"Miss me?" Gideon asked, looking way too pleased by her forwardness.

"A little." She'd surprised herself. She wasn't known for spontaneity.

"Hop on," he said as Ed took off toward the building.

She climbed aboard and set her arms at his waist, his jacket thick and cushiony. They didn't have far to travel. Her hair didn't even get messed up. "You owe me a real ride sometime," she said as they climbed off.

"Deal. I have several snowmobiles for my business. We'll plan a day trip. How'd it go?" he asked quietly as they headed into the building.

"I'll tell you in the car."

"It's bad?" he asked, his voice instantly tense.

"You two want to stay for dinner?" Ed asked, poking his head out the door at them as they neared.

"We have to get back to Sacramento tonight," Gideon said. "But thanks for the offer."

Twenty minutes later they loaded the model in the car and headed out, with about a half hour of daylight left.

"So?" he asked.

"She might recognize me, once she thinks about it some more." She told him what had happened. "It's not like I was a movie star, where people might still be watching videos of me or something. I should be gone from the public's memory. But there's no guarantee."

"Well, we can't do anything about it except hope if it would make a difference to her that she doesn't make the connection until after the deal is done." He reached over and laid his hand over hers. "Were you in a panic?"

She sniffed. "I never panic."

He smiled. "Good to know."

"Even though I learned today that I'm a skiing fanatic—which I'm not, by the way—I'm extremely close to my family, I'm happiest at home and I want four children?"

He looked a little contrite. Just a little. "Did I tell her we wanted four children?"

"Apparently so."

"Sounds like you covered well."

"Maybe. She frowned a lot at some of my answers, so I had to backpedal. I'm sure I came across as ditzy."

"I'm sorry."

"Honestly, Gideon, I felt really guilty at pulling the wool over their eyes."

"I know. But listening to them talk, you got the impression of what they want, right? Someone who loves the place and will keep the wholesomeness of it. If they sell to me, they're selling to someone who believes in the same things. I'm just not married."

"I understand what you're saying. It's why I was so nervous about messing it up for you."

"I appreciate that."

"However, she said something else that surprised me, although maybe you're aware of it. You have a mutual acquaintance? Jake McCoy?"

"Seriously? I've known him all my life. His brother Joseph is my brother David's best friend."

"She mentioned him as being the only other person from Chance City who she and Ed know. Apparently he skis there quite a bit, although he hasn't been this season."

Gideon drummed his fingers on the steering while. "This could be a problem. Jake's the one I want to ask to take over my business for a while."

"Do you think you should take him into your confidence? Before he accidentally learns we're married and says something to your brother?"

"I don't know. I have to think about it. I really don't want to include anyone in the lie except you and me. Much safer that way. Anyway, he's out of the country at the moment." He gave her a quick glance. "Nice touch at the end, by the way."

"What touch?"

"When you raced up the snow bank to welcome me back. Very convincing newlywed moment."

She hadn't planned it....

And there was no way was she telling him that.

Chapter Five

Gideon pulled into his driveway an hour later. They'd stopped talking a while back. It hadn't been uncomfortable, but as if they each needed to regroup. He knew she was worried about her notoriety causing problems with the Bakers, but he thought the chances of that were slim. He also had no control over it, so he let it go. He had enough to worry about, like how he was going to find an investor.

After being out on the mountain in the snow with Ed, Gideon wanted The Trails more than ever. It was exactly right for him. And he would finally prove that he *could* amount to something, that he wasn't a daydreamer, but someone who could follow through and succeed. Not that his father would ever know—and not that Gideon wasn't successful now. Still, he was driven to succeed in this venture in a way he'd never been before, maybe even more so. With Max dead, Gideon was starting almost from scratch. The challenge excited him, even as time was closing in.

He parked and shut off the engine. Denise smiled at him, a kind of sleepy, sexy smile he hadn't seen from her before. "You'll stay for dinner?" he asked.

"I'd love to." She stretched. "I need to wake up before I drive home."

They got out of the SUV. She headed toward her car. "I brought a folder with info we can discuss on investors. I made notes last night."

He loved to watch her walk, so he lingered, enjoying the view. She exuded a simmering passion. It was in the way she moved, the way she looked into his eyes, the way her mind worked. And the way she laughed, low and sexy.

She had big dreams for herself, and he admired that, but he also knew it would be a roadblock to taking their relationship further than this deal. She would have to move to San Francisco to open a new branch of her business, then Los Angeles, she said. His own plans would require his full attention, as well.

But there was that attraction, that fire between them—

"You're quiet," she said as she returned and they walked the path to his stairs.

"Sorry."

She cocked a look at him. "I'd much rather know what's on your mind. Are you upset about the whole thing with Joanne?"

"No." Silence was probably better than telling her he was fantasizing picking her up, carrying her into his house and dropping her on his bed, not letting her out of bed for hours. "I was trying to remember what I have in my freezer," he said. "I made some soup and corn-bread the other day. Does that work for you?"

She didn't answer right away. "Sounds good," she said, her tone indicating something other than assent.

He built a fire while she thawed and heated the soup, then they took their bowls and sat on the sofa to eat, the fire roaring. For the first time all day she'd taken off her sweater. Underneath it was a pale green, form-fitting, long-sleeved T-shirt that didn't appear to be cotton but something soft and silky. They'd both taken off their boots. She stretched out her legs, her feet toward the fire, and wriggled her toes inside thin, white socks. A file folder lay on the sofa next to her, as well as a small notepad.

She balanced her soup on her lap and tore out a sheet from the notepad, then passed it to him. "I was standing in the parking lot trying to imagine the hotel, and this popped into my head. I can do a more detailed drawing at home later, but I wanted your input. I know they aren't the minor changes I was talking about before, but I think this is better. Obviously we need to talk to an architect."

"Explain it to me."

She spent the next few minutes sharing her vision, ending with, "Do you think it's doable?"

"I'm not an expert. It looks good, but I still think it's too late to get another architect involved. Madigan took more than two months to get the first plans done. He had to scope the land, get engineering reports, those environmental impact studies."

"I know someone who could come up with something in a couple of days," she said, "based on this drawing and Madigan's reports. As I said before, you don't need full blueprints, just renderings."

"And an accurate estimate of costs. We can't present a ten-million-dollar plan when it's more like twenty."

"I have an architect in mind—Cicely Stevens. She's good, really good."

"Do we need permission from Madigan?"

"You said you hired him to create the plans. You haven't entered into a contract with him to build it."

"It was understood." He liked Denise's design, but he was a man of his word.

"Would it hurt to give it a shot? I'll keep your name out of it, if you want, so there's no possible way he would know. It's your whole future, Gideon, not just business."

She made a strong case. "Aside from this pretend marriage, I'm always honest about my business dealings. I would want to meet with this new architect myself. But I'd only make the change if she can guarantee it would take only a couple of days. We need the design to show the investors, and we can't delay any longer on that."

"Speaking of which." She picked up her file and opened it. "I made up a list of people with the kind of money you need. I'll show you mine if you'll show me yours." She batted her eyes.

He laughed and went to get his list, then passed it to her. "As I told you, two have shown interest enough to schedule appointments on Wednesday—Tom Anderson and Robert Copperfield."

"I know of them, of course, but haven't met them," she said. She took a bite of corn bread and studied his list of names. "I don't know any of these people personally."

He went down her list. "Who's this Gabriel Marquez? Why does his name ring a bell?"

"He's a world-famous artist but also a big-time venture capitalist. He and his wife became clients a few years ago. They live in San Francisco. Cristina, his wife, and I have become good friends, beyond the business. I could call her."

Gideon didn't know how he felt about that, was having a hard time letting her be involved beyond the role he'd planned for her. But time was running out, too. "Yeah, okay. Why not?"

Her finger on the number listed on her sheet, she reached for his portable phone on the coffee table.

"You're calling them now? On a Saturday night?"

"It's worth a shot. They've got three kids under ten, so maybe they'll be home."

"Sounds like a good reason to be out," he murmured.

Denise laughed as she dialed. "Cristina, hi. It's Denise. Is this a good time to talk? Okay. Well, I've got a favor to ask. You know I don't like to play the friend-ship card, but my husband—"

She met Gideon's gaze. He saw her hesitate at the lie, then she forged ahead.

"Yes, you heard that right. I'll explain it later, okay? My husband and I are looking for an investor, and I thought of Gabe." She relayed the pertinent details of the deal then said, "Sure, thanks."

She covered the mouthpiece. "She's talking to Gabe."

Gideon didn't like sitting on the sidelines. He was all for equality between the sexes, but this didn't seem equal. Plus she'd had to tell someone she was married.

He hadn't expected anyone she knew personally would become involved in their lie. He should've thought it through better.

"Really?" she said into the phone. "Let me check." She held the phone against her chest. "They want us to come to dinner tomorrow night. Gabe has a friend he'd like to involve, too, a Ben O'Keefe. Apparently he owns quite a few hotels. What do you think?"

"The new hotel design won't be done by then."

"We'll wing it." She grinned, the excitement in her face coming through in her voice, too.

It was what he wanted, so why was he hesitating? "I'm free."

She talked into the phone again. "We'd love to come, Cristina… Sure. Six-thirty is great. Thanks so much." She hung up and sat back, looking pleased.

"You told her you were married."

She frowned. "That's our strategy."

"Won't that be hard on your relationship with them? If Marquez invests, he'll be involved for the long haul, and you—both of us—will come off looking like a couple of flakes when we get a divorce in a few months."

"Don't worry about it."

"Why not? I don't want you—or your company—to get hurt because of me. Reputation is critical in business."

"I'm a big girl, Gideon. This is my choice. I'm not going into it blindly." She set a hand on his fist, resting on his thigh. "I should probably get going. I'll need to get in touch with Cecily first thing in the morning so that she can get busy on the new hotel design."

"Not without me."

"Of course not. Do you want to drive down early?"

He mentally considered contingencies. An idea took hold. "I've been thinking about Jake knowing the Bakers. If he does come back and happens to see them, and they say something, it's probably better that we already have the appearance of a marriage going on."

"Meaning what?"

"That we should be living together."

She smiled in a way that said, "Oh, really?"

"That's a long commute for me, Gideon. Unless you're talking about moving in with me."

"I could do that."

Her gaze was direct and heated. He had no idea what it meant.

"All right," she said. "That makes it easy to meet with Cecily early tomorrow, plus we've got to get to San Francisco by six-thirty, anyway. Everyone else on your list is local, right? You might as well figure on staying for the week."

It would be a test of his willpower. He liked testing himself. "That's a generous offer, thanks," he said finally. "I should go pack a few things." He needed a couple of minutes away from her, too. Should they establish new rules now that they would be living together?

"I'll do the dishes," she said, as if she was happy for a few minutes to think, too.

"Denise," he said, stopping her. "I need to say something. I'm not sure I can without sounding ungrateful or chauvinistic. Or arrogant."

"Okay. I'm warned."

"You need to remember that this is my plan, my dream, and I make the decisions, ultimately. I know you're a strong, decisive woman, used to being in charge yourself." He saw her retreat, not physically but mentally.

"What are you saying?"

"I want you to see the big picture. There's time to change your mind. I can cover about you with the Bakers."

She crossed her arms. "Maybe you should spell out the big picture for me as you see it."

"Aside from my need to lead this deal, there's the fact that anyone who gets hooked up with it will think you're part of the package. Are you willing to risk that? It could lose you clients at some point—like Cristina Marquez—if the deal doesn't fly and she finds out you were less than truthful."

"Cristina's more my friend than client. As you say, no one will ever know the truth unless we tell them. So, I'll seem a little flaky? I can deal with it."

He hadn't thought she would be reckless. Maybe the image she'd created and perpetuated for herself as Denise was hiding the fact she was still the woman called Demi, a risk taker, an adventurer—the kind of woman he generally was attracted to.

He moved closer to her. She didn't budge. "There's also the chemistry between us. Have you thought about that? If we give in to it, it could change everything, at the very least our personal relationship. I've never been a fan of mixing business and pleasure. It's usually the surest way to disaster."

Her expression softened from looking ready to argue to understanding. "Gideon, I do understand that what you originally wanted from me and what you're getting are at odds. I did get caught up in the moment. I've settled into a routine at work, and I hadn't realized how much I missed the excitement of growing something new." She put a hand on his arm. "But I'm fully aware that this is your plan, and you're the boss. I'll try to be a little more…wifely."

He smiled at the image. "So tomorrow night, if the men want to retire and talk business, you'll be okay sitting with the wives in another room, talking about whatever it is women talk about?"

He saw something in her eyes that took his smile away. Some deep down hurt that he knew better than to ask her about, no matter what she'd said about honesty. Whatever it was, it was probably part of the reason she'd run away from her past life. Maybe when she trusted him more, she—

"I'll do whatever you need me to, Gideon."

"As long as you get credit after the deal is done and your fee."

Her eyes took on a teasing glint. "Tiny though it may be."

"But worth every potential penny."

She laughed. "Potential. The key word."

"I only accepted an offer you put forth," he reminded her. "I'll go pack so that we can get on the road."

When he was almost done packing, she peeked into his bedroom from the doorway. Her gaze landed on his bed.

"Do you ever fall off that dinky thing?" she asked, pointing to the massive California king bed.

"I like space."

"Obviously." She wandered in and strolled around the room, picking up a framed photo from his dresser.

"My mom," he said. "Virginia."

"Are you close?"

"Yeah. Now. We weren't for years. I was pretty ticked off at her. She and my father divorced when I was four. He got sole custody. It wasn't until he died that my mother and I built a real relationship."

"What do you suppose she would say about this pretend marriage?"

"That it's a better choice than the real thing."

"Where does she live?" she asked, registering surprise but not continuing with the hot topic.

"Las Vegas. She's a Realtor." He set his suitcase and garment bag by the door and went to stand beside Denise. He pointed to the other three photos. "David and Noah and me when we were kids. David's wedding, as you can tell. Noah and his family. I'll have to get something more current with Tricia in it. Noah's wife died three years ago. Plus the children have grown up a lot since then."

"You were a cute kid."

"I was an unhappy kid, but I smiled for the camera, like most kids do."

"I didn't see your brothers' names on your list of potential investors."

He walked away. "You won't, either. No hard feelings. We just keep our businesses separate." It wasn't the whole truth, but if she could keep her secrets, he could keep his, the ones from the past, anyway. Some secrets didn't affect their relationship, either personal or professional.

She followed him out the door. "I don't know, mountain man. You may feel claustrophobic in the mere queen-size bed in my guest room. Could be a tight squeeze for you."

He turned around and gave her a look. "I'd be fine with sharing *your* bed."

"What? So I won't worry about you falling out of bed?"

"I'm an old Boy Scout. Always prepared. And only thinking you might rest easier."

She laughed. "Generous of you."

"I can be that, too."

She didn't miss a beat. "Good thing, since you've decided I can be demanding."

He couldn't read her expression, unusual for him. Either she was exceptionally good at hiding her feelings or he wasn't as intuitive with her as he was with most people. "Are *you* generous?" he asked.

"Definitely. Are *you* demanding?"

"Only one way to find out."

She put a hand on his chest. He tried not to react too much.

"Maybe when our deal is done we can," she said.

"If we last that long." He couldn't help but notice how her nipples pressed against her silken T-shirt like an invitation. He grabbed his luggage. His pretend-marital rights weren't clear yet, legal or personal, but he knew this wasn't the moment to test them. "Let's go, Mrs. Falcon."

He smiled to himself, liking how his calling her that shook her up a little every time. And since he wasn't going to get sex anytime soon, he had to do *something* to entertain himself.

Chapter Six

On Sundays Denise usually rolled out of bed, made a pot of coffee, grabbed the newspaper from outside her door and spent an hour or so on the sofa enjoying the morning. This Sunday she had to brush her hair instead of winding it at her nape, and dress in sweats instead of just pulling on a robe.

She wasn't complaining. The reward for her change of routine was that Gideon slept in the room next door. She hadn't heard any noise during the night, so if he snored, it wasn't loud. And she'd been awake more often than not, so she would've heard.

She liked having him there.

She wondered what he thought of her condo and its contemporary, colorful furnishings, a setting so different from his comfortable, masculine, rustic home. The only similarity between their places was that both their kitchens had granite countertops and stainless steel appliances, although her cabinets were sleek and cherry, and his were knotty pine.

Denise made her bed and drew back her drapes. She spotted him on the balcony that ran the length of her unit, down both bedrooms and the living room. He'd pulled on jeans but that was all, even though it was only about forty degrees—which meant it was ten degrees warmer than where he lived, so it probably felt almost tropical to him. His hair was sleep-mussed. Why was it men could get away with that and they looked great, even adorable?

She opened the slider and joined him.

"Morning," he said, heat in his eyes—or was it wishful thinking on her part? He passed her his coffee mug, which he'd doctored with cream and sugar, the way she liked it. He drank his black.

She could get used to being pampered.

"Perfect, thank you," she said after tasting it. She tried to pass it back to him but he gestured that she should keep it. "I didn't hear you get up," she commented. "Or noise from the kitchen."

"I *am* a tracker, you know."

Which was why he'd surprised her a couple of times last night before they'd gone to bed. He'd just seemed to appear next to her.

She sipped the coffee and watched him study the cityscape while she studied his well-muscled arms and bare chest. "Aren't you cold?" she asked.

"A little. Want to warm me up?"

She held out the mug, and he laughed. "I fixed that for *you*. I'll go get my own."

They went in through the guest bedroom. His

bedding was jumbled, one pillow on the floor, the other smashed against the headboard.

"Bad night?" she asked as they passed through.

"Actually, I slept really well. Why?"

She gestured toward the bed.

"I dream a lot," he said, as if that would answer the question but actually only prompted more in her head. "And don't worry. I don't expect you to clean up after me. Noah trained me well. He was like a master sergeant in our house." He eyed her as he scooped up a T-shirt from atop the dresser and dragged it over his head. "I'll bet your bed is neat and orderly when you wake up."

He was right. In fact, her bedding was usually so undisturbed she could just pull it up, plop her decorative pillows on it and be done.

"No comment?" he asked, laughter in his eyes as they made the turn into the living room then entered the kitchen. "Guess I hit the nail on the head. Are you insulted?"

"I figure it's a sign of a clear conscience."

"Really? I figure it's a sign of a dull life."

She shoved him playfully, and he laughed. She wished he hadn't put on a shirt. It had been a long while since a bare-chested man had hung out with her, and this particular man had a much nicer chest than the average.

He poured himself a mug of coffee from the pot he'd made, then topped hers off. "So. I checked out your refrigerator. I thought you liked to cook."

She took the gibe gracefully. "I do. I generally plan my meals a week at a time and buy what I need. Today would be my normal day for that. Stacy and I meet for brunch most Sundays, then I shop after." She opened her refrigerator and looked inside, then checked her freezer. "I make killer Belgian waffles."

"Works for me." He sat at the bar while she pulled out ingredients, including a bag of frozen strawberries to make a chunky sauce. She poured the contents into a pan, added some sugar and a splash of water, then turned the burner on low. She took out her waffle iron and plugged it in.

"When will you talk to your architect friend?" he asked.

"I already have. I texted her last night, and she answered this morning. Said we could come to her place at eleven. If that's okay with you," she remembered to add, not used to having to run plans by him.

"Sure. She lives nearby?"

"The penthouse, one flight up."

"That's convenient."

"Cecily introduced herself in the elevator the day I moved in a couple of years ago. She throws the best parties, always an eclectic mix of guests, a number of whom have become clients." Denise measured out flour as she talked. "She and I often hang out after work together. You'll like her, I think. She's in her early fifties, very short steel-gray hair, almost-black eyes, always wears something fluid and flowy. She's the most naturally beautiful woman I know."

"But have you seen her work?"

"Of course."

"Has she designed any hotels?" He got off his stool and came around the counter into her space, then stirred the fruit as she mixed the waffle batter.

"Not that I know of, but she's brilliant."

"What's her expertise?"

"Restoration."

He raised his brows.

"I know," she said. "That doesn't mean she can't design something from the bottom up. She sounded excited about the project."

"In a text message?"

She bumped a hip against his. "Yes."

"If you say so." He lowered the heat a little then opened her freezer. "Do you mind if I cook up some of these turkey sausage links?"

She hadn't thought about his needing a heartier meal and some protein. She'd only been interested in showing off her own cooking skills. "That'd be good, thanks."

"And maybe add some lemon to the strawberries?"

She laughed at his intentionally humble tone. "Who's the chef here?"

He tossed a lemon at her that she was somehow able to catch. She couldn't remember ever having so much fun in the kitchen.

They mostly talked recipes and best-ever restaurant meals until breakfast was done and the dishes were put in the dishwasher. They each took showers and dressed. Gideon was sitting at her kitchen counter reading the newspaper when she finally joined him.

"Is this strange for you?" she asked.

He looked up from reading the comics. "What?"

"Not being able to see your trees?"

He continued to look at her, a slow smile forming. "I like this view just fine."

Heat rushed to her face.

He picked up her left hand. "You haven't taken off the ring."

"I'm afraid I'll forget to put it on when I need to, like tonight." Which was a complete lie. She was aware of it every second, would be aware of it on the chain, too. It was like a little branding iron wherever it touched her.

"I think you should take it off for this meeting. She's your friend, not an investor. It'll keep the lies to a minimum."

He'd already taken off his ring, she noticed, so she followed suit. He stood behind her and undid her chain, slid the ring onto it then refastened the clasp, letting the ring slide into her cleavage, as he'd done the first time, his fingers brushing her nape, his body heat a welcome sensation down her back.

His proximity tempted her. She'd known it would when she invited him to stay with her, but she hadn't figured on it being never-ending. She hadn't set herself up for this kind of temptation before. The relationships she'd had were as she'd told Gideon—straightforward and uncomplicated, usually ending amicably. She was coming to realize that a parting of the ways with Gideon would be hard. Maybe too hard.

"Ready?" he asked.

"Let me get my keys."

Gideon watched her walk away then picked up the scale model, his gaze landing on the miniature hotel. He still had doubts about switching architects so late in the process, but he also liked Denise's ideas. She had good taste, as evidenced by the elegant decor in her condo. Not surprisingly, it was extremely neat—and she hadn't even known he'd be coming home with her. Neat freaks were generally control freaks, as well. He'd seen her in charge, but he'd also seen her let go, too, and give in to her feelings, so he was hopeful that she could be more flexible than he suspected.

Several times during the night he'd wondered what she would do if he woke her up. He wondered if she slept—

"All set," she said, a copy of the plans in her hands.

"Do you sleep naked?" he asked, then enjoyed her startled reaction.

"Excuse me?"

"I figure it's something I should know, in case Joanne asks."

She got that look on her face he was coming to know well—that you've *got* to be kidding look.

Still, she answered him. "Joanne was curious about a lot, Gideon, but I doubt very much she would get that personal."

"You never know. So? Do you?"

She sighed. "Yes. Do you?"

He nodded. "Satin sheets?"

Her laugh was low and beguiling. "No, but supersoft percale. I love the feel of that fabric against my skin."

Yeah, he would've liked slipping under the covers with her and finding her naked and ready. "A yes or no would've sufficed."

"You started it." Her smile widened as she held the front door for him. "I'll try to remember that you need things kept simple."

"Brat," he said but enjoying her.

Silence settled between them on the quick trip to the penthouse. He would've liked to back her up against the mirrored elevator wall and strip her so that he could see her from every angle as he made love to her. Come to think of it, the guest room's three closets, which took up an entire wall, were mirrored. He wondered whether the master bedroom was the same.

He gave her a long, speculative look as the elevator doors opened on the next floor.

"I do believe I've just been undressed with your eyes," she said, a slight hitch in her voice.

"It's not the first time." He walked past her as she held her arm across the door so it wouldn't shut on him, then she followed him.

"You know we're just making things harder on each other by talking about it, admitting things like that."

"You said to tell you the truth, Mrs. Falcon, remember?"

"I remember."

They'd reached the front door of one of the two penthouses on the floor. She knocked. He found it interesting that she hadn't fired back a comment.

The door opened. Denise had described Cecily perfectly, but her condo was a surprise. For someone whose expertise was in restoration, who must have a love for old things, her home was even more modern, more austere, than Denise's.

"You must try this absolutely divine espresso cheesecake," Cecily said after the introductions. She picked up two plates with servings already cut. "Here. Eat. Let me look at what you've brought."

Gideon was game for a good cheesecake anytime, but his stomach rebelled. He wasn't a professional model builder, and she was used to expert work. And then there was the fact he was still uncomfortable bringing in a new architect at this point.

Denise huddled with Cecily, answering questions, explaining her drawing of the hotel, her vision.

"And you, Gideon?" Cecily asked after a while. "This is what you want?"

He set aside his barely eaten cheesecake and approached them. "I like her ideas."

She tapped a finger to her lips. "An evasive answer if ever I've heard one."

"If we had more time to work with it, I would say yes, this is what I want. But we have very little time."

Denise put her empty plate on the tabletop. "Maybe the Bakers would be okay with an extension."

"Unless I'm the only one bidding, I doubt that would happen. They're ready to move on."

Denise nodded. "I get that feeling about them, too. Well, what do you think, Cecily?"

"I can get you a rendering and probably an estimate within twenty percent of actual by Tuesday night. Is that good enough, Gideon?"

Both women looked at him, waiting.

"I have moral and ethical dilemmas about this," he said, "as I've told Denise. I'm sure James Madigan expects to be the architect in charge of building the hotel. How would you feel," he asked Cecily, "if a client accepted your plans, then turned around and hired someone else?"

"It's happened to me. It's just business."

"I don't do business like that."

"Would you rather have a nondescript hotel that guests don't remember?"

Her question hit him hard. "That's a rhetorical question, I assume. Is there a compromise?"

"Probably not to your satisfaction. I think you're admirable. I do. But Denise is right. What you've got is fine but ordinary. To dazzle an investor—and eventually guests—it needs to be extraordinary in order to compete. You can do something that looks more awesome for close to the same amount of money. It's your choice."

He wandered away from the women, went to stand at the big picture window with the same view as Denise's. He let his gaze drift over the skyline. The more unusual buildings caught his eye, making him linger and study them. Most structures he passed over. It gave him his answer. But he would call Madigan himself and let him know. That seemed not just fair but necessary.

"Okay," he said aloud. "Create something memorable."

"And if you could have a drawing by five o'clock that we could take with us to San Francisco, that would be fabulous," Denise added, making Cecily laugh.

"You're a pushy broad."

"You've known that for quite a while now."

"Yes. And now that you've got me working on a Sunday, you'd better scram so that I can get to it. I'll give you a call when I've got something good enough to show off. By the way, Gideon. Your scale model? Nice job."

"Thanks. And thanks for taking this on with such short notice."

"Technically you're taking me on, since I haven't done anything like this in at least twenty years. I'm eager." She walked to the door with them. "So, how did you two connect?"

Denise met Gideon's gaze for a second before she answered. "I told you about two recent clients, Noah and David Falcon, who hired employees from me then fell in love? Gideon's a Falcon brother, too. We met at David's wedding."

"Oh, so you're the one she could've danced all night with," Cicely said, turning her attention on him, singing the words as if she were Eliza Doolittle.

Ahh. So, Denise had even talked about the evening with her friends, he thought, enjoying how her cheeks pinkened at being caught. He almost teased her about it, then, oddly, it struck him that she wasn't wearing heels today, making her seem shorter, and more vulnerable for some reason, and he didn't want her to be uncomfortable in front of her friend. "It was *my* pleasure," he said.

"And a gentleman," Cicely said. "All right, I've teased enough. Go forth, and enjoy your day."

"So," he said as they waited for the elevator, "what'll it be? Go for a walk? See a movie? Christmas shopping?" He tried not to shudder at his last suggestion. He hated mall crowds.

"I can't believe you're not going to mock me. I'll bet you didn't tell a soul about us dancing all night."

"You'd be wrong."

She looked at him sharply, as if she didn't believe him.

"Noah and I had a talk about you." Mostly he'd been wondering why she dyed her blond hair brown, although he'd also admitted to being intrigued by her.

They entered the elevator. She pushed the lobby

button. "A walk sounds great to me, thanks. We can go out to the river, then shop for groceries on the way back."

Good. He wanted to see her environment, and it was a crisp day, perfect for walking, although they probably should've stopped by her place and picked up sweat-shirts or something. She seemed not to notice the cold.

"So, will Noah tease me if I see him again?" she asked as they fell into step in front of the building.

"Noah? Tease?"

She laughed. "Well, I figure he's lightened up, now that Tricia's in his life."

Gideon shrugged. "Maybe. I haven't seen him a whole lot in the past couple of weeks. Do you have siblings?"

"A brother. Trevor. Heir apparent to the family business."

There was bitterness in her tone, another piece of the puzzle about why she'd checked out of the paparazzi life she'd led. "You're not close?"

"We were as kids. I'm just a year older. I haven't seen him lately." She looked at Gideon. "I would love to be as close as you and your brothers are."

"We're not always in sync."

"But you're always there for each other. That counts the most."

She was right. It did. They had a unique bond, perhaps, because of how they'd been raised—together, but each of them having a different mother, their bullying father their common enemy. "You said you aren't estranged from your father, but you aren't close, either. What does that mean?"

Her jaw hardened. "It means I see him now and then, talk to him now and then, e-mail now and then, but neither of us goes out of our way to make it happen."

"What about your mother?"

"I see her more frequently. She flies up here and spends a weekend occasionally. We talk a couple of times a week. In many ways, Cecily fills that gap for me. And she never tells me to behave myself."

Her fragmented relationships obviously hurt her, but he didn't know to what to degree, or if she could recover from it. People often hid their feelings, never letting on how much they hurt.

"Do you misbehave often?" he asked, taking her hand in his, a little surprised when she clutched his harder instead of resisting, not surprised at how cold she was.

"I try." She smiled at him, but she seemed fragile, a word he wouldn't have used to describe her until now. "I'm not very good at it."

He'd researched her on the Internet and wondered how she'd survived the kind of attention she'd gotten. He would've knocked out a few teeth, himself.

She'd looked like a wraith, nothing like the healthy woman of today. And her friend of the co-headline "Deni and Dani" was just as thin, as gaunt, really, although not quite as vulnerable looking.

"Your old friend, Dani?" he asked. "Did you cut off contact with her, too?"

"I had to."

"Does she know where you are?"

"If she does, she's never contacted me. You know what? It's a beautiful day, and I don't want to talk about this stuff anymore." She pulled out a twenty-dollar bill from her pocket and stuffed it into a red kettle, wishing the bell ringer a hearty Merry Christmas.

The more Gideon came to know her, the more depth he saw. She was very good at surface control, but he knew by the way she squeezed his hand that her emotions were running high.

He'd never considered himself an overly protective man. He hadn't learned that from his father, or even his mother. And certainly not from Noah, who had taken on the parental role, even if not by choice. Gideon had come to realize that Noah, four years older, had tried to prepare him for life, for the real, hard world.

But every protective instinct Gideon had—and some he hadn't known existed—rose up when he was with Denise. He didn't want anyone to hurt her. It was unrealistic, of course. But as long as he was around, he would be her safe harbor. Her rock.

He would make her laugh, too.

It was the least he could do for someone trying to make his dreams come true.

did any such thing. Cia—[illegible] when I saw that her _____ from even a decent _____ to _____ _____ she just wasn't into it, into her relationship. We'd _____ out loud ___ ___ too, when the two of us ___ ___ [illegible]

had no idea ___ the _____ _____ for _____ her reputation ___ _____ mint _____ ____ that tonight. It wasn't going to ____ _____ to her to tell him the truth: she __ ___ ____ in love with _____ _____ _____ every moment. But Gideon's _____ _____ _____ ___ [illegible] money. His _____ ____ _____ to her _____ _____ _____ _____ _____ [illegible] ____ clear. He'd _____ ___ [illegible]. _____ it was ___ [illegible].

Chapter Seven

For all that Denise had told Gideon she didn't mind lying to her friend Cristina Marquez, it wasn't entirely true—just another necessary lie. She did mind. She *was* nervous. This was a friendship she valued. Cristina had recognized her right away when they met. And they shared a common bond—Cristina having grown up in the spotlight, too, her father a senator. She was a beautiful, voluptuous woman in her early forties, her hair a gorgeous red-gold.

"Our wonderful chef, Jean-Paul, created this meal in your honor, Denise. He says you'll understand," Cristina said as their entrée was served later that evening—spaghetti and meatballs that would be anything but ordinary.

"We spent one entire afternoon talking food before I sent him to you to interview," Denise explained, cutting into a tender, perfectly browned meatball. "He recited his recipe for spaghetti and meatballs, and I made him promise to make it for me someday." She took a bite and closed her eyes. "Mmm. Even better than I imagined."

"You picked out the perfect person for our family. He's giving our children a wide range of food experiences," Cristina said. "I hope no one lures him away."

"He adores you, *bella*," her exotically handsome husband, Gabe, said. "He's not going anywhere."

Conversation flowed during the meal, from food to travel to polite politics and more—six people with varied interests, tastes and points of view. The Marquez's stunning Pacific Heights house was decorated top to bottom for Christmas, all sparkly and bright, taking Denise back to her childhood when Christmas had been a big deal.

Gallery-quality art dotted the walls—Gabe's own work and that of others he admired. The house could've seemed like a museum but didn't. There was nothing stuffy about it, and it was evident that children lived there.

With a promise of dessert to end the evening later, Denise watched with envy as the men went off to Gabe's office to talk, while the women retired to a second floor room overlooking the neighborhood. Framed photographs of Gabe and Cristina's wedding, as well as their three children at various ages, took center stage on a gleaming black piano. The wedding photo included the other pair of dinner guests—Ben and Leslie O'Keefe.

"You've been friends a long time," Denise said, trying to keep herself from leaving the women in the dust and invading the business meeting. She hated being left out of the loop.

"Ben and I have known Gabe since the first day of high school," Leslie said, taking a seat. She was a tall, slender woman with short chestnut hair. Her Ben was very tall, very broad, very handsome—a lot like Noah.

"How long have you been married?" Denise sat in a wingback chair facing the women, who sat on a small sofa.

"Twenty-two years. Minus three." Leslie smiled at Denise's confusion. "We took a little break for a divorce at one point."

"True love never dies," Cristina added.

"Not to mention the small matter of getting pregnant out of wedlock. Both times." She grinned. "But, yes, true love."

"Cristina told me you and Ben own some boutique hotels," Denise said, not asking the personal questions on her mind.

"Yes, twelve of them, all long-stay properties. I understand you're well versed in the hotel business, as well. We've met your parents several times."

Denise felt as if a giant claw had picked her up and slammed her into a wall. She glanced at Cristina, who picked up on her shock right away.

"Was that supposed to be a secret?" Cristina asked, leaning toward her. "I know we didn't discuss it much before, but I always figured you just weren't trading on your father's name for your own success. I would've done the same thing, would've needed that pride of accomplishment in my own right."

"No, it's fine," Denise lied. "I was just surprised. I

guess it is a small world, this hotel business. Do you socialize with my parents?" she asked Leslie.

"Me personally? Rarely, and only in group events. Ben does, however. After 9/11 we became part of a charity to help victims in New York. We met your parents because of that. Frankly, I was too in awe to talk to either of them, but Ben never lets awe get in the way. That's why he's so successful. The hotel business is all his, really. Although, honestly, I can't promise Ben hasn't said anything. I admit I didn't have a clue who you were until Cristina explained. Now, if you'd been on the Most Wanted list…" She smiled.

Denise made herself laugh. Leslie was a homicide inspector for the SFPD.

"This project of yours wasn't new to Ben, either," Leslie continued blithely, not realizing how much she was shaking up Denise's world. "Ben talked to the Bakers—is that their name? He heard the property was for sale. But apparently they will only sell to a couple who'll continue what they started, and Ben's all about change."

Denise felt hollow. So now Gideon's friend Jake McCoy knew the Bakers, as did Ben and Leslie, who also knew her parents. How much more complicated could it get? Now she and Gideon were really stuck in the lie about being married. No turning back.

A small, quiet women came into the room. "Excuse me, Mrs. Marquez."

"Yes, Yolanda?"

"Mr. Falcon is asking for Mrs. Falcon to join the gentlemen."

Denise hopped up. She'd been trying to figure out

how to change the subject, afraid to get herself in deeper, if that was possible. Gideon had been right about keeping the lies to a minimum—right, but also living in a fantasy world.

She followed Yolanda to a large, masculine office down the hall, all dark paneling and deep colors. The men stood at her arrival. The distinctive scent of cigar smoke lingered, although none of them were smoking at the moment. She tried to picture Gideon smoking a cigar and couldn't.

He came toward her. The look he gave her was a caution of some kind. Then he hugged her and whispered, "Keep an open mind."

She'd had enough surprises for one evening.

"Ben has a couple of suggestions," Gideon said to her as they all took seats. He'd been wondering how flexible she was. He was about to find out. He hoped she would speak to him after. She already looked a little strained.

"Nothing structural," Ben said. "But a couple of trends I've spotted lately that you may want to incorporate."

As Ben and Denise talked about timeshare versus points and buffets versus full menus, Gideon reran the comments Ben and Gabe had made, the questions they'd asked, trying to decide whether Gabe was leaning toward saying yes or no. Smart businessmen asked good questions, hard questions. Gideon felt he'd answered them all, and frankly, he'd anticipated every possibility. He'd been living and breathing this project for so long that he knew it like a lover, inside and out. He could find a statistic in a twenty-page document blindfolded, just like a man knew the perfect spot on his lover's body to send her soaring.

Watching Denise spar—politely—with Ben gave Gideon an even greater appreciation for her. Velvet and steel. She was a fascinating mix of both.

Which is why he knew she would be both demanding and generous in bed....

"So, the ultimate question," Ben said to Gideon but including Denise. "Do you plan to build a brand to take elsewhere? Or are you putting everything into The Trails only? Is this the end of the road?"

"I can't give you a definite answer," Gideon said, aware that Denise was just as interested in his response. "Once this is up and running, I might want to do it again somewhere else. But I have an even greater need right now to settle down and have a family. I don't want to be an absentee father."

He was surprised at how still Denise had gone. Maybe they hadn't talked much about his personal goals—nor hers, for that matter. They'd discussed her goal of opening more branches of her own business, something he had a strong feeling had more to do with her relationship with her father. Then, of course, there were the goals they'd made up for the Bakers.

"I can tell you from experience that it doesn't take that much time," Ben said. "It's more a matter of finding the right people to run things."

"I'm a hands-on guy. Not sure I'd be happy turning over the reins to anyone else."

"All right," Gabe said in a tone that seemed to end the discussion. "I hear that Jean-Paul has made an incredible dessert in Denise's honor." He stood, and everyone else followed suit. "Once I have the new estimates on the hotel, I'll make my decision."

"Is your father in on the project, Denise?" Ben asked.

Gideon saw her stiffen. He answered before she could. "I asked her not to involve him as yet. We'd both like to make it on our own."

She slipped her hand in his and squeezed it, then addressed Ben. "I understand you and my father know each other. It might be good if you don't tell my parents anything, because—" she glanced at Gideon "—we eloped. And we haven't told them yet."

Ben hesitated, surprise on his face. "Well, I wouldn't have, even without your asking. I did get an e-mail from him today, though, and when I responded I told him that Leslie and I were having dinner with you tonight."

They all moved through the doorway and headed to the room where Cristina and Leslie waited. Gideon wondered about the specifics and the consequences of that e-mail.

Yolanda, carrying a laden tray, came up the stairs as they moved down the hall, a chef-jacketed man behind her. His face lit up.

"Denise!"

"Jean-Paul!"

They both-cheeks kissed. Jean-Paul and Denise kept the reunion short, but Gideon watched her mood lift—especially with the chocolate tiramisu the chef had created.

Gideon and Denise didn't linger too long after that, were back on the road to Sacramento by nine-thirty. Neither spoke for a while. He hoped by being silent that she would tell him what was on her mind.

"I thought I would be an asset to you, Gideon," she

said finally. "I think not only am I not helping, I'm making things worse."

"In what way?"

"You've got a new architect at the last minute."

"I could've said no."

"One who hasn't ever done a project like this."

"My decision to say yes, though."

"Yes, but now you're under an even tighter crunch while we wait for plans."

"Again, Denise. My choice."

"And we have no idea if Ben told my father he was having dinner with me, or with me and you, or with me and my *husband*. I should've asked. Now I don't want to call and ask him, to give it that much importance. I think he would've told us if he'd included your name, don't you?"

"Probably. Maybe we'll find out the answer to that when we get back to your place, in the form of a voice mail or e-mail. Or possibly him waiting on your doorstep, demanding to see my financials to know that I can take care of you." He smiled at her, trying to ease her mind—and his own. Lionel Watson had the power to interfere in Gideon's minor-by-comparison project if he wanted.

"He'd better not show up unannounced," she said.

The tension in her voice made him consider what his relationship with his own father would have been had he still been alive. Probably even more tense than Denise's with hers.

"Do you think Ben thought it was weird that we weren't including my father in the plans?" Denise asked.

"From what I gathered, Ben built his business from

blood, sweat and tears. He would respect us for wanting to do the same," he said. "Here's something else I found out, however. Ben knows the Bakers. Was interested in buying the property until he found out they weren't qualified by Ed and Joanne's standards."

"Leslie told me. I don't think it'll matter, since they're not in contact. It *is* a small-world thing, though."

"The point is, if Ben knew, a lot of people knew."

"Which means there could be a lot of bids for The Trails," she said quietly, looking straight ahead.

Their conversation stopped after that, then when they got to Denise's condo, there was a message on her machine from her mother. "Your father told me you were to meet Ben and Leslie O'Keefe tonight. They're a lovely couple. We're curious about how you hooked up with them, of course. Give us a call when you get in, all right, dear?"

"Are you going to?" Gideon asked.

She hit the erase button. "No."

"What do you think? Do they know something?"

"It wouldn't surprise me a bit if they knew I had a man living with me. My father can afford to pay for information. If that's what he's been doing all these years, I've been pretty dull material." She finally looked at Gideon. "As for the business or marriage aspect of it, I think it's possible my father knows something is up but not specifics, which is why my mother called—to feel me out. To get answers to gentle motherly questions."

"You can't avoid them forever."

"I can avoid them for a few days. They know I'm always swamped this time of year."

"Do you go home for Christmas?"

"No. They send presents, and my mother will come up here soon after."

"What do you do Christmas Day?"

"Spend it with friends. I assume you're with your family?"

"Yeah. It's a zoo, but a happy one. Should be even better this year."

She turned away and headed for the kitchen. "I'm going to have a cup of tea. Can I get you something?"

He would've told her to go change out of the stunning little black dress and very high heels she was wearing while he fixed tea for her himself, but he decided she needed to do something.

"Ice water, thanks," he said. "I'm going to change into something more comfortable, if you don't mind." He hadn't worn a suit, but dress pants and shirt and a sports coat.

"Those loafers hurting your feet?" she asked, a smile in her voice.

He was glad to hear it. "I'm still breaking them in."

"Yeah? How long have you owned them?"

"Six years."

She laughed. "Poor baby. I'll give you a foot rub."

He looked at her, wanting to know if she regretted an offer made while she was teasing him, but she started filling a tea kettle, her head turned. Massages could be highly effective foreplay. Was that her goal?

He changed into a T-shirt, sweat pants and, after a short internal debate, white athletic socks then returned to the kitchen just as she was dipping a tea bag up and down in hot water.

He wondered if she knew how sexy she looked doing

the domestic task while wearing the figure-hugging black dress and spiky heels. Incredibly sexy.

She glanced at his feet as he approached then raised her brows in question.

"I wasn't sure you were serious," he said, picking up a glass of ice water from the counter where she'd put it.

"I was serious."

"Seems like you would be the one in need of a foot rub. Doesn't it hurt, wearing those shoes?"

"The price of beauty." She grinned. "And ego, I guess. I like how I feel in them."

"Sexy?"

She shrugged.

"You succeed," he said, leaning his elbows on the counter, watching her move to the sink to throw her teabag into the trash can beneath it.

Maybe he should just go to bed. Get away from her. He wasn't going to be able to hide how aroused he was, not only at the view before him, but at the thought of her hands on his bare feet. Maybe if they talked business at the same time… .

She walked past him, a mysterious smile on her face, as if she knew her power over him, then sat at one end of her sofa. "Lie down," she said, patting the cushion next to her.

"You don't want to change into something comfortable, too?" he asked.

She kicked off her shoes. They toppled on top of each other. Her skirt had slid to about five inches above her knees. "Done," she said.

He set his glass on a coaster on the coffee table and

stretched out, putting his feet in her lap, letting her decide whether his socks should be on or off.

She tugged his sweats up a little and peeled off his socks, dropping them on top of her shoes in a kind of erotic still life, then ran her hands from his ankles to his soles. He swallowed a moan and closed his eyes, deciding to enjoy the attention. He was generally the pursuer in a relationship, was good at romancing, and unsure about letting a woman take the lead, at least early in a relationship.

But not this time. He didn't know what made it different for him, why he was not only letting her take the lead but okay with it. In truth, she was the worst thing that could happen to him at this point in his life. He was finally in a position to get himself on the path he'd been wanting. He would have a business that could keep him at home most of the time and still be doing the kind of work he loved. And he would finally have time for a family.

However, he couldn't have that with an accomplishment-driven woman who had her own goals, her own drive to achieve. She'd scheduled her life.

In that sense they weren't a good match, wouldn't be good for each other, but there was no denying their chemistry was white-hot.

Her hands felt wonderful. Her fingers pressed into his insoles, tugged on his toes, stroked his insteps. Opening his eyes to slits, he caught her staring at his hips. He liked that she was looking. He closed his eyes again, an involuntary groan escaping.

"Feels good?" she asked softly.

He sort of laughed. "You could say that."

"Keep your eyes closed and try not to react too much."

Heat suffused one foot—she'd pressed her mug of tea against his sole, then held it there for a while before she worked the muscles for a good long time, repeating it with his other foot. It was a new experience for him, relaxing him completely, especially when she stroked his feet over and over.

"You're not ticklish," she said.

"No." He forced his eyes open and stretched. "Sorry. I almost fell asleep on you."

"That would be okay. I like doing something for you. You're not good at letting me. What's with that, anyway?"

"Wanting to lighten your load is a bad thing?" he asked, sitting up. He sat close to her, rubbing shoulders amiably, their thighs almost touching.

She smiled. "When you put it that way, no."

"Okay then. Thank you for the foot rub."

"You're welcome." She took a sip of tea, looking at him over the rim, but he couldn't read her expression.

He was losing his touch. He should be able to figure her out, especially when she looked at him directly. "A personal question for you," he said.

"Okay." She took another sip. A nervous reaction?

"I've been looking at you all night but I haven't seen bra straps."

She put a hand over her mouth, her eyes going wide. Finally she swallowed her tea and laughed. "All night, huh?"

"Absolutely. From the moment you stepped out of your bedroom."

"And you looked hard?"

He stared at her, and she laughed. "High and low," he said.

"Well, maybe you didn't succeed because I'm not wearing a bra."

He dropped his gaze and studied her until she bumped him with her shoulder. "You would've been swaying, if that was the case," he said. "You weren't. Believe me, I checked."

"I'm wearing a kind of…corset, I guess you'd call it. It's strapless."

He wanted to see it. He'd admired the swell of breasts above it all night. "Is it comfortable?"

"The price of beauty," she said, as she had before.

"Why do you do that to yourself? Why not just be comfortable? Or does it make you feel sexy, too, like the shoes?"

"Yes." She looked away for a minute then faced him directly. "I've never been with a man who asked so many personal questions."

"Does it bother you? Are things moving too fast?"

"I don't know how to answer that, since I don't know where this is going to end up, only where it's headed at the moment."

"We're both feeling our way through it. There's no need to rush, is there? We need to stay honest with each other—that's what we promised. The buildup is good, too." He meant it—and yet he didn't mean it. In theory, he liked the buildup, the foreplay, the anticipation. But in practice? In practice he wanted to carry her into her bedroom and not sleep all night.

But for all her celebrity background, he had a feeling that she wasn't as worldly as most people might assume. Innocence often shimmered in her eyes, or maybe more naïveté than innocence, a lack of experience in romantic relationships. She could handle anything in business, of that he had no doubt.

"Yes, the buildup is good," she said finally.

"So. High heels and a corset make you feel sexy. Which begs the question of what else you've got on underneath your dress."

"Does it?"

He heard a smile in her voice and was glad of it. "Yeah."

"Thong. Garter belt. Stockings."

Blood rushed from his head. Everything below his waist throbbed. He could no longer come up with a logical reason for why he shouldn't sleep with her.

She patted his hand. "Are things moving along a bit too fast for *you?*" she asked sweetly.

"I've been trying to be sensitive."

"That's an unusual role for you?"

No, he thought. He was probably known for that, but in a detached sort of way. As an advisor or something. People always asked his advice. "I haven't been in this situation before—working with someone I'm attracted to. But we're talking about a relatively short period of time. We should be able to keep the attraction under control."

"Not if we keep flirting and teasing the way we do."

He nodded, agreeing.

"I'm not trying to see if you have a breaking point, Gideon," she said, standing and heading to the kitchen.

"I know the relationship is complicated."

"You want to hear complicated? Leslie and Ben have been married for twenty-two years, minus three. They got a divorce at some point, then remarried. And she was pregnant both times they got married. Relationships are complicated, period. Frankly, I like that ours is."

She said that now, but would it be the case if feelings deepened and she had to make decisions about the goals she'd been working toward for five years? Would it be the case for him, too?

He'd had a hard time believing that his brothers had fallen in love as quickly as they had… .

Love? It was a ridiculous word to use in this situation. If they fell in love, one of them would probably have to give up some dreams, and he wasn't about to do that. Not now. Not when he was so close. On schedule.

And if there was one thing he knew for sure about Denise Watson, it was that she would reach her own goals, too. Which meant parallel paths for them—and never the twain shall meet.

Chapter Eight

Denise hoped her condo was empty when she got home from work an hour early the next day. She didn't know exactly when Gideon would turn up, but she hoped she would have at least an hour to get things ready—or mostly ready.

Finding that Gideon was still gone, she called down to the lobby and told the delivery men who'd arrived with her to hurry upstairs. While she waited, she moved a side table from one end of her couch to a spot a few feet from her fireplace, then she scrambled to the door when she heard someone approaching.

A man in blue jeans and a Santa jacket and hat came straight into the room, carrying a four-foot, fragrant Scotch pine, a teenage boy behind him hauling shopping bags.

She thanked them several times, tipped them well

and immediately went to work decorating the tree. She'd chosen the tree on her lunch hour, asked them to add lights and a stand, then deliver it, along with the ornaments she'd bought earlier.

She'd been happy all day. She'd caught the Christmas spirit in the Marquez's house the day before. Seeing everything so bright and shiny had made her realize how little she'd decorated during the past few years. Candles, a few trinkets, some garland, a needlepoint stocking from her childhood and that was about it—and most of that only because she had an open house the first year she'd moved in.

Not this year. This year Gideon would be there to enjoy it, too. She wanted to surprise him. She'd even bought new holiday CDs and played them while she decorated the tree. Finally she stood back to admire her work then rushed into the guest room, where she stored the rest of her things.

She was on her knees, headfirst into the closet, when someone said, "Nice view."

Denise dropped her forehead to the floor in resignation. She hadn't taken time to change, wanting to be done when Gideon got home, so he'd caught her with her rump in the air. She'd had to pull her skirt up to her hips to maneuver herself into the corner of the closet. Her hair had fallen out of the clip she'd used to keep it out of her face. She pictured him staring at her backside, knowing she couldn't back out gracefully.

"Are you having fun?" she asked as she moved backward.

"Absolutely. Are you?"

She heard laughter in his voice. Relax. Go with it, she told herself. You can have fun with this, too. "The most I've had in ages." She emerged. He was there, his hand out, offering assistance, which she took.

"You got a tree," he said once she was standing. He hadn't let go of her hand.

She blew a wisp of hair from her eyes. "I wanted you to have a little bit of home."

He kissed her lightly, sweetly. "Thank you."

She felt herself smile idiotically. She was proud of herself, happy that he appreciated her efforts. It had been so long since she'd done anything like this.

"Can I carry anything?" he asked, and she piled his arms with boxes, then brought the remainder herself.

They entered the living room, and she stopped cold. A tree stood in the space dividing the living room from the dining room. It had to be eight feet tall. Gideon looked at her with suppressed amusement. Pine scent permeated the space.

"We had the same thought," she said, not knowing how to react, not knowing his reason for bringing it. She'd intended hers as a gift to him. He could've been pleasing himself by bringing this tree.

"We can put mine in the lobby," he said. "Leave a sign on it—free to good home."

"Of course we're not doing that. So we'll have two trees. So what? Maybe it's a reason to throw a party or something." Her thoughts swirled. She was suddenly, totally into the idea. "New Year's Eve."

Silence fell between them. If everything went as planned, they wouldn't have any reason to be together beyond Christmas. They would present the bid on Christmas Eve, then the Bakers would say yes or no.

Well, she could have the party regardless, couldn't

she? Maybe she would need a diversion of that magnitude at that particular time. Except she would have to make a decision now, issue invitations, make plans.

"I hope you brought ornaments," she said, pulling her hands along a branch, releasing more fragrance from the soft needles. She held her hands to her face and sniffed. "This is really fresh."

"It should be. I chopped it down this morning on my property."

"Ah. Mountain man." She pictured him wielding his ax, the muscles in his arms and back bulging from the effort.

"Where would you like me to put it?"

They moved a decorative chest into her bedroom so that the tree could take center stage in front of the floor-to-ceiling window. Yes, he had brought decorations, he said. They were in his car. He went off to get them.

A phone rang, the ring tone not hers. She spotted his cell phone on the dining room table and went over to look at the screen. "The Trails," it said. She opened it.

"Denise Falcon," she answered.

"Denise, this is Joanne Baker. I'm glad it's you. If I'd known your company's name, I would've tracked you down there, talked woman to woman."

Her tone was all-business. Denise's heart slammed into her chest. "Is something wrong?"

"I'm not sure exactly, but I'm pretty confused, enough so that Ed and I have made a decision. He wasn't going to tell you and Gideon, but I don't want anything hidden—which is part of the problem. Apparently we can't say the same about you and Gideon."

"Pardon me?" Denise moved to the door and looked through the peephole, watching for Gideon.

"We learned this afternoon that you've hired a new architect, have a new plan."

"It just happened, Joanne. Just. And only for the hotel." How did they hear about it? Who could've told them? And why? "We decided to go with a more innovative design, something memorable. We'll show you the plans, I assure you."

"Well, that's not exactly the point. Obviously Ed and I don't have a say in what you do with the property, but Gideon has been so open about everything, until now that is. We were so sure he would take into consideration the clientele we've built through the years, and not price them out of coming here. Keep it family friendly, you know?"

Implied in Joanne's words was the charge that Gideon hadn't *lied* until now—now that Denise was his wife. "That *is* his plan, Joanne. What do we need to do to prove that?" She spotted someone walking down the hallway, then let herself breathe again when she saw it was her neighbor.

"Ed and I spent the afternoon discussing it. We even called our daughters and talked to them. One son-in-law is our accountant. They all feel we should open up the bidding without requirements, see what the potential is."

So, it was coming down to money finally. They *could* be bought. "I assume you're extending the deadline, then?"

"Only by a week, to New Year's Eve. Ed and I want to finish up here. I know that's probably foolish. We should give it more time, but we're even more anxious now and ready to make the move. I guess you could say we've had an attitude adjustment. So we'll accept bids only, no plans necessary, because as we've just learned, it doesn't make any difference, does it? Someone can say one thing and do another."

"Gideon wasn't going to do that. The change of architect happened last night. He planned to show you the new design."

There was a long pause, then Joanne said, "Well, there's also the other detail we learned—about *you*. We know who you are, Deni Watson. Why didn't you tell us?"

Denise closed her eyes. So there *was* a connection in the Bakers' minds about her coming into Gideon's life and him lying to them. Her fears had come true. "Does it really make a difference?" she asked, but already knowing the answer. Apparently it made a huge difference.

"A wife's influence on her husband is substantial," Joanne said.

"I'm sure you're right. But how do you think that would change the end result? I have no more interest in creating a celebrity playground, as you put it, than you and Ed."

"Ed believes otherwise. Anyway, I wanted to tell you. Be straightforward."

Two figures were headed down the hallway. She recognized Gideon's walk. Cecily was beside him. "I appreciate that, Joanne. We'll have our offer in on New Year's Eve, as planned."

Denise hung up and returned his phone to the dining room table, where he'd left it, then she opened the front door. Gideon looked at ease and happy. She hated to steal that from him.

"Dinner," he said, hefting a box containing a slow cooker, from which came a heavenly fragrance. "I ran into Cecily in the garage and invited her to join us, but apparently she has a date."

Cecily was carrying several sacks and her briefcase. She set everything down. "No 'apparently' about it. I have a date with Simon Moore," she said to Denise. "He finally wore me down."

"Good. I like Simon."

Cecily opened her briefcase and pulled out a folder. "I called in every favor owed me on this. I've never used so many estimators on one project. Anyway, here it is. It doesn't include approvals and permits or other incidentals, but it's a good ballpark figure for the hotel itself. It's not too far from what the other was estimated to be." She headed toward the door. "I've got to get ready. I don't remember ever having a first date on a Monday before. It's throwing me off my game." She flashed them a smile and left amid thanks from both of them.

Gideon set the slow cooker on the kitchen counter, then lifted a smaller box from one corner. With a satisfied smile, he passed it to her. The thought of snatching that excitement from him was painful to her.

"Here's how I spent most of my day at my cabin," he said. "Open it."

Inside a layer of bubble wrap was a scale model of the new hotel design, right down to the indoor/outdoor, winter/summer swimming pool with the retractable glass walls.

"It's fabulous." She swallowed, tried to smile. "You're quite the Renaissance man, aren't you? Chop down a tree, make dinner, build a model. Just an ordinary day in the life of Gideon Falcon."

"I wouldn't say ordinary, but I had fun." He grabbed the folder Cecily left. "Let's see what she's come up with."

They sat at the dining room table and examined the numbers together. Finally he said, "The cost is five percent higher, but I think the concept is unique enough that an investor would be more willing to open his wallet. What do you think?"

She closed her eyes for a second. "I think we have a problem."

Gideon blew out a breath and sat back after Denise broke the news—the door was now open for anyone to buy The Trails.

It was a huge blow.

"Any guesses on how they found out about the change in architect?" she asked.

"A couple of possibilities come to mind. How about you?"

"Yeah, maybe. What're yours?"

"I called James Madigan this morning and told him I was going with a different architect. He didn't take it well."

"In what way?"

"Probably in the same way I would've, had the situation been reversed. We had an implied deal."

She was quiet for several seconds, her hands fisted on the table. "I'm so sorry. I shouldn't have done anything except what you asked of me. For you to go back on your word like that must hurt."

More than he could tell her. However… "Cecily's concept—no, *your* concept—is better. There isn't even a lesson learned here. In the same situation again, I would do exactly the same thing. But now I'm thinking that Madigan could be the competition, or maybe some friend of his. He very well could've decided to pursue it on his own. Unfortunately he's got hard numbers, the environmental impact study, everything. Wouldn't require much last-minute running around. He's even met the Bakers, having gone to the site to check it out before designing the hotel. And if all someone needs is a bid, a week is enough time. Hell, they could win the bid and turn around and sell the place for a profit, probably." He shoved away from the table and went to plug in the slow cooker to reheat dinner, needing to get up and moving.

"Did you have another idea?" Denise asked.

"You heard Cecily yourself. She called in favors. Maybe one of those *favors* spread the word to someone."

Denise frowned. "That's a long shot."

"I know. In any event, what happened can't be changed. It all comes down to money now." He stirred the pot, releasing the aromas from the still-warm pot roast, potatoes and carrots, his favorite winter meal. "You said you thought of something, too?"

"What we talked about last night. I figure when Ben e-mailed my father, he probably talked about meeting me and my husband, a perfectly natural thing to say, since Ben doesn't know the truth. And hearing that shocking news could've started my father on an all-out investigation, especially when I didn't call my mother back. He would've taken matters into his own hands after that."

"Would he really be interested in building an adventure resort? Watson hotels are luxurious. The Trails area can't sustain clientele like that. Surely he would see that right away."

"That doesn't mean he wouldn't get into the game, for the fun of it."

It was a strange kind of fun. "Why don't you just call your parents and see what they wanted? If they found out you're married, you can set the record straight."

"And have that information reach the Bakers? For sure they wouldn't sell to you. Too many lies." She came up behind him and gave him a hug.

He turned, pulling her against him, needing to hold on. "Tangled web," he said.

"More like mangled. It's all my fault."

"Ever heard of free will? It's not your fault." He tucked her closer. As much as he liked seeing her in her high heels, he liked holding her when she was barefoot. Her head fit against his shoulder perfectly, her face pressed to his neck. "So, if your father tracks *me* down, you want me to stick with our story?"

"I don't think we have a choice, but it's your baby. I'm going to let you take care of it the way you want to. I've *helped* enough."

"I have no issue with how you've helped, Denise. Stuff happens. But I don't know about your relationship with your father and why things are so complicated."

She moved back and looked him in the eye. "My father gave me the opportunity of a lifetime. He'd decided to buy a small chain of mid-priced hotels, to create a less expensive, more business-friendly offshoot, aimed more at management-level clientele than executive. He put me in charge of the remodeling

plan—which is how I got to know James Madigan. I had
to work closely with him on the project."

"I take it you didn't get along."

She moved out of reach and leaned against the
counter, her arms crossed. "To put it mildly. I called his
ideas stuffy. He didn't like that."

Gideon smiled at the image. "How old were you?"

"Twenty-two, fresh out of college."

"And cocky."

She shrugged. "Confident."

He laughed. "I'll bet."

"I looked around his office at the photos of his
designs and everything looked cookie-cutter to me. I
thought if my father wanted to appeal to a new market,
he should have a new look."

"He didn't agree, I gather."

"He is a strong believer in not fixing what doesn't
seem to be broken. Tends to be reactive instead of pro-
active, or at least as he's gotten older. Since it contin
ues to work for him, how can I argue? But this was a
whole new game." She looked off into the distance.
"Madigan went straight to my father to complain.
Instead of standing up for me, or hearing me out, or
giving me time to prove myself, he fired me."

Her father sounded a lot like his own. "Then what?"

"Ironically, he put my brother in charge. Trevor is
famous for accomplishing things on charm alone. He
didn't make waves, sucked up big time and all the men
were happy. And get this—they ended up using my
plans. Obviously I wasn't charming enough."

"Makes you wonder if it had more to do with your
being female. What did you do?"

"Went a little crazy. That was the heyday of Deni and Dani. I partied. And I hurt. I tried to find work, but I was untouchable. I don't think my father had anything to do with that, but no one in the business took me seriously—or they saw me as a spy or whatever—and given the headlines, who could blame people, anyway? That's when I made the decision to drop out of the fast lane, move here and start something of my own. I couldn't look at myself in the mirror anymore."

"You should be proud of yourself."

"I am, thank you. I'll be prouder still when I have my own empire to dangle in front of my father."

Gideon thought it sounded more like a vendetta. He also figured it had a lot to do with The Trails and that hotel. She wanted to show her father she could build a hotel. She was already a success in her own field, but this would be the hotel business. Part of her deal with Gideon was that she got recognition. It had to be to impress her father, whether or not she was admitting that, even to herself.

"My point is, Gideon, if Madigan found out I'm involved in this project, it makes sense that he would try to interfere. Or that he would call my father and let him know. Something. He hated my guts. I was the only person to stand up to him. A young, know-it-all upstart, and a girl at that."

"So, is that the real reason why you vetoed the hotel design and wanted a new architect?"

Her face flushed but she met his gaze directly. "No. Well, maybe that was a small part of it. But I would never let personal feelings get in the way of good business. It wasn't the showcase it needed to be."

"Okay," he said after a minute. "Let's eat dinner and finish decorating. No business talk allowed until we're done."

"You're not sorry you involved me in this?" she asked, her hand on his arm.

He shook his head, although it wasn't the truth. He was sorry. Just not for the reasons she thought. They should've met another time, another place—when it had nothing to do with business. He wished he'd come to that realization before now. Because now there was no turning back.

Chapter Nine

Denise hadn't lied to Gideon, she just hadn't told him everything, hadn't told him that the Bakers knew who she was. Before she did, she needed to talk to Ed and Joanne. Which was why she left Stacy in charge the next morning on an overwhelmingly busy work day to make the long drive to The Trails. She didn't call ahead, figuring the Bakers would be there. She didn't want to give them any warning.

There were fewer cars in the parking lot, but since it was a Tuesday, she assumed that was normal. Over the next two weeks, when most of the schools were on winter break, they should see full lots and trails.

She parked and headed for the office, looking up at some ominous clouds as she went. She didn't have snow tires or chains, so all she could do was hope that she could head back before any serious weather hit. Gideon had a meeting late in the afternoon with Tom Anderson, whom he'd been courting awhile. He wanted her with him for that.

An overhead bell jingled as she stepped inside. Joanne was manning the counter, talking to a customer. She waved at Denise.

"Help yourself to some coffee in the dining room. I'll be with you in a bit," Joanne said, returning her attention to her customer.

Denise took her coffee with her to stand at a window and looked out at the snow-covered vista. It really was beautiful, a place where you could hear yourself think, breathe fresh air and forget about the world. She pictured the new hotel and trails. It wouldn't overwhelm but draw people to its serenity, while still being filled with adventures for all ages and risk levels. Summer would be just as beautiful, in an entirely different way.

"Can't say I'm surprised to see you," Joanne said, coming up beside her. "Does your husband know you're here?"

Guilt niggled at the word *husband*. "No."

"Did you tell him about our conversation?"

"Yes. Just not the part about you recognizing me. Is Ed around?"

"He's on the snowmobile, patrolling the course. It's just as well, I think. We should probably talk this over between us. Let's go to the conference room, so I can watch the desk, too."

Denise wondered why it was just as well that Ed wasn't there, but she didn't ask. She was fine dealing directly with Joanne, who seemed the most reasonable but who could wield her influence. They sat in the same places as they had—was it only three days ago? A lot had happened since then.

"First of all," Denise said, "I'm not here to ask you to change your mind about anything or to plead a case. I just want to set the record straight about me and my past, because it shouldn't reflect poorly on Gideon, who is the best, most moral and ethical man I've ever known." If they didn't count the lie about marriage, she thought, a small white one, in her opinion. "He didn't have to tell Mr. Madigan that he'd decided to use a different architect, but he did tell him. I assume it was Mr. Madigan who told you?"

"Does it matter who told us?"

No help there, Denise thought, disappointed at still being in the dark about who'd talked. "I guess it doesn't. What matters is your opinion of me—what's real and what's rumor. Gideon shouldn't have to pay a price for my past."

Joanne smiled slightly. "Husbands and wives are connected. What one does, the other has to deal with. You haven't been married long, and you're the product of a different generation, but you'll come to see that in a good marriage, it's the partnership that counts the most. You each assume each other's burdens and triumphs, their pain and joy. That's when you know you've got yourself a real marriage."

It was a wonderful definition of marriage, a humbling definition. "Thank you for the wisdom, Joanne. I do appreciate it. You're right, we should be connected, and certainly we are in this project. But he's a little blind, a little idealistic when it comes to me. He didn't believe my past would or should have any bearing on the business of this project. I knew he was probably wrong." Denise folded her hands in her lap and looked directly into Joanne's eyes. "All I'm asking is that you listen to my side before you decide Gideon's not worthy because of me."

Denise wasn't going to get into all the details of her past, of course. What happened within her family was their business, no one else's, but she could explain her transformation.

"I was a spoiled little rich girl, I admit. But in my own defense, you have to understand that that's the way I was raised—with privilege and luxury but also with the threat of kidnappings. It's a very strange way for a child to live, but I knew nothing else."

"I can only imagine."

"I love the hotel business, Joanne. I worked at The Watson Los Angeles starting in my early teens, got my degree in hotel management. But there were different expectations for me—people demanded more than they would have from another employee, or they didn't want to work with me at all. Things got rocky, and I had to leave. Then I didn't know what to do with myself. It had been my only goal since I was a child."

Joanne patted her hand. "I know it's hard to live up to a parent's dreams."

Not in this case, Denise thought. It had been her dream for herself that was shattered. "I admit I had a couple of wild years, along with my friend Dani."

"Oh, Ed told me all about her. She's still a wild one, I gather."

Denise hesitated. "Ed did?"

"He's the one who's into the Hollywood stuff. Buys all the magazines. He's the one who recognized you."

Stunned, Denise sat back. She was talking to the wrong person? "Does he tend to believe tabloid headlines?"

"I guess so, since he reads them to me and shakes his head."

"So, he probably doesn't believe it when that celebrity says there's no truth to the matter. Or there's only enough truth to give it a shocking headline."

"You know how men are."

Denise didn't think you could lump all men into one heap, but she couldn't say that. "What shocked him the most about me? Did he say?"

"Apparently you've been out of the scene for too long for him to remember the specifics, just that you'd been a lot of trouble. Something about getting drunk one night and wrecking a car into some fancy restaurant?"

"Not me. Someone I was with," Denise said, recalling the horror. "But I shouldn't have let her drive." Wouldn't have, if she'd been sober herself. She'd reached the bottom of the barrel that night. It'd been her turning point. No one had been hurt, except Dani lost her license, and the building had to be repaired. "There's a difference between Deni and Denise, Joanne. A huge difference. I built a successful business on my own. I'm responsible and reliable. I'm not Deni anymore. And, frankly, Gideon wouldn't have been interested in Deni, either."

"You talk like you're not even related to Deni."

"In many ways, I'm not. I still have a strong work ethic, however, and a need for success. That hasn't changed. In fact, if that computer behind you is connected to the Internet, I'll show you."

Joanne studied her for a few seconds, then spun around in her chair and logged on. Denise came around the table, searched her name and easily found a photo of her and Dani from five years ago. She stepped aside to let Joanne look.

"Goodness. You don't look anything like that now." She stared hard at Denise, then back at the photo.

"I've changed as much internally as externally."

"And you want me to assure Ed of that?"

Denise smiled. "You said wives have influence. I would've included him in this discussion had he been here. I'm not hiding my past from either of you. I just didn't want you to think Gideon also had something to hide. I want you to know, he's a good man, true to his word. And so am I. He wouldn't have come here to defend his name, so I had to do it for him."

"I think he would've come here to defend *your* name, however. Good husbands do that, Denise."

Joanne was right. Denise had gotten so caught up in trying to persuade Joanne of Gideon's worth and countering her own rumors that she'd actually ignored the pretend marriage in her own argument. She also realized how inexperienced she was regarding marriage. How easy it had been to say yes to a pretend marriage when she didn't really know what marriage entailed. Yes, Joanne was right about a lot.

So, now the lie was growing as the list of people involved grew. She and Gideon were in too deep to stop, though. She couldn't interrupt his dream. It was his concept, his—

She stopped the thought as she realized how much it had come to matter to her, too. And not just because he had agreed to her involvement regarding the hotel part of the plan, beyond the negotiations. She was hooked on the whole idea.

And him. Especially him.

"I don't think there's anything else I can say, Joanne. I appreciate the time you gave me."

"Will you tell Gideon about our conversation?"

"Yes. Will you tell Ed?"

"Yes. He needs to know the whole picture. But I'm afraid it's not going to stop us from hearing other offers, Denise. The kids have convinced us that we'd be foolish not to get the best price, to secure our retirement. They've always thought we were foolish about the married-couple thing. And I haven't changed my mind completely, but they have convinced us to at least see what else there is."

And their children wanted to secure their own inheritance, Denise added mentally, a fact worth considering. There was nothing wrong with that. "It's sensible advice, of course, but I hope it's not your only criterion, not after all your years of hard work," Denise said, standing and holding out her hand.

Snow started to fall during the drive home, big, fluffy flakes, nothing heavy enough to prevent her from making her way back to Sacramento in time to get some work done before the four o'clock meeting with Tom Anderson.

She wondered how Gideon was going to react to what Joanne had told her. Last night had been very different from the night before, when she'd given him a foot rub and they'd flirted with each other. Last night they'd decorated his tree and the rest of the condo, holiday music replacing conversation most of the time.

Then they'd sat down to make a new plan, without the intimacy of the previous night, just business. How much would the offer have to be now, given the competition? They already had to bump it up to adjust for the new hotel estimates. More than that, even?

Gideon had driven to San Francisco this morning to hand deliver the estimates to Gabe Marquez and to show him the new model of the hotel. She hadn't heard yet how that went.

Denise parked in her condo space then walked the few blocks to her office. Several phone messages awaited her, including one from her mother. She would return calls after she met with Stacy to see what had happened during the five hours she was gone, something that rarely occurred.

But when she got to her office, she found Gideon sitting there. And he didn't look happy.

Gideon liked surprising people, because it generally gave him extra insight into what made them tick. Denise smiled, greeted him then sat behind her desk, setting a stack of while-you-were-out message sheets next to her phone.

"How'd it go with Gabe?" she asked.

"I'll tell you in a minute. How've you spent your day so far?"

"Productively. I had a meeting away from the office."

"I'm guessing it's one we should discuss?"

She raised her brows.

"You've got the wedding ring on," he pointed out. "And you never wear pants to work. So let me take a wild guess and say you went to see the Bakers."

She pulled off the ring and lifted the chain over her head. "I was going to tell you."

"Were you?"

"Yes. Absolutely." She got up and closed her office door, then sat in the chair next to his. She launched into a dialogue about how her reputation was dogging him, dragging him down, just as she'd suspected it might, and ending with her hope that she'd gotten through to Joanne.

It didn't sit well with him that she'd taken over like that, made that kind of decision without him. "Why didn't you tell me this last night?"

"Because you wouldn't have let me go. Or maybe you would've gone on your own and argued with them, defending me." She slipped her hand into his. "It was better coming from me. I hope they respect me for it, and therefore, you."

He saw her point—to a point. "We should've gone as a team. It would've had more impact."

"Joanne would agree with you," she said with a smile. "For now, it's best if they think it's me, not you. Especially after our 'divorce.'"

He hadn't thought about that, and he should have. He'd gotten entrenched in the lies, enough so that he forgot about them most of the time. "Gabe's strongly leaning toward saying yes."

Denise cheered, then she wrapped her arms around him and kissed him. What started as celebratory turned into something else, intense and almost desperate. He wanted to bury himself in her, feel her skin against his, see her face when she climaxed. He'd already been waiting more than a month for that, even though most of that time he'd resisted calling her. The difference now was he wanted to wake up beside her in the morning and watch her sleep….

He held her arms and moved back. "'Strongly leaning,' I said. We've got a long way to go, but I feel cautiously optimistic."

Denise's eyes lit up. "That's great."

"We'll see. Maybe Anderson or Copperfield will give a quicker answer."

"One day at a time, Gideon."

"Deadline's coming fast. No time to rest. Although more time now than we'd expected." He stood. "I'm going back to your place and make a few calls. I'll meet you at Anderson's office, okay?"

"Four o'clock, on the dot."

He started to leave then turned back. "Thanks for what you did today."

"You're welcome."

"Don't do it again." He knew she knew what he meant. He wasn't being a dictator but someone who needed teamwork from her. If this was going to succeed, she needed to trust him. They needed to trust each other.

He didn't like how she just smiled a little at him without assuring him she wouldn't take matters into her own hands, but he was going to trust in the fact she would do the right thing.

Chapter Ten

Two days later Gideon found himself at loose ends. Until the people they'd wined and dined and wooed gave him answers, he was stuck. There was no one else to contact, not with so little time left, and Christmastime at that. He was surprised that Gabe Marquez hadn't given him an answer yet. And he felt good about Copperfield but not Anderson, except Gideon knew Denise had wowed the man. She'd sparkled, had even changed into a classic but sexy business suit and her equally sexy high heels.

Since Denise was working, he took himself to the Falcon Motorcars headquarters in Roseville, just north of Sacramento. The company rarely had outside visitors or clients, the deals usually being made away from the office and shop, frequently in Europe, which meant they didn't need a receptionist. What they had was Mae

Carruthers, Noah's assistant, who had been the primary administrative assistant since Aaron Falcon had started the business over thirty years ago.

"Well, look what the wind blew in," the red-headed Mae said with a smile. She gave him a big hug.

He tried to remember how long it had been since he'd visited. Years, certainly. Five? Six? Nothing had changed, from the sound of pneumatic tools in the shop to Noah and David arguing a point in Noah's office beyond Mae's desk.

"Go on in," she said. "Surprise 'em."

"Need a mediator?" he asked from the doorway. It'd been worth the step back in time just to see the looks on their faces. Because they had the same father, there were similarities between the three of them, but the DNA from different mothers mixed it up a bit. Noah, four years older than Gideon, was the tallest, broadest, and most serious. David, three years younger, joked the most and tended to go with the flow but could be intense and aggressive when necessary. Gideon's talent had always been in dispensing sane advice and wisdom. He could use a little of that himself at the moment.

Neither brother made a move to greet him. They looked at each other, then back at Gideon. "What's going on?" he asked, coming into the office.

"We were just about to put in a call to you to ask that very question," Noah said.

"Give him a chance, Noah," David said, the words conciliatory but his voice cooler than Gideon could remember hearing. "I assume you came to tell us your news?"

How had they heard about it? "It's not a done deal yet."

"That's not what we heard," Noah said.

"I don't know where you're getting your information, but I haven't kept you in the loop because you said you weren't interested."

"Not interested in who you marry? What makes you think that?" Noah asked.

Marry? A string of curses ran through Gideon's head. How the hell would they have found out about that? "Who told you?"

"Tom Anderson." Noah gestured toward his telephone. "He called to ask if David and I were part of the deal you're putting together. It was difficult enough answering a question about something I knew nothing about, but then he went on to say what an amazing wife you had. Let me tell you, it wasn't easy not blurting out, *what wife*? I kept asking questions until he finally said her name—Denise. Not too hard to put two and two together."

"I tried to tell you about my deal—at David's Labor Day party, in fact. You didn't want to hear about it."

"Right. *That's* what we're interested in hearing about," David muttered.

Gideon was stuck. Should he tell them the truth? Noah wouldn't approve—that was a fact. As for David, maybe he could be convinced, but it would take an exceptional debate.

Gideon didn't want to deal with it right now, not when he was so close. "I was going to announce it at Christmas," he said finally. "I didn't want to steal your thunder, Noah. Yours and Tricia's."

"We haven't even set a date yet."

"Well, we didn't want to wait." He shoved himself up and walked over to look at a photo of his father. Most people thought it was there in tribute, but his sons knew it was there as a reminder to live differently.

"When did this…event take place?" David asked.

"The night you got married."

Complete silence followed for several long ticks of a clock.

"After spending about three hours together?" Noah asked.

"We'd actually met the week before, remember? At David's bachelor party. I told you then to keep your hands off her because she was mine."

"You did?" David said to Gideon. "How come no one told me?"

"Did you see her during that following week?" Noah pressed. "I recall you and I had a discussion about her during the reception. You never once mentioned having seen her. All I remember you saying is that she intrigued you. Something about her being a blonde and dying her hair brown."

"Really?" David asked. "Is that true? Why would she do—"

Gideon turned and faced them. "Nothing matters but the fact we went to Reno and got married."

"Without inviting us?"

"You'd just left on your honeymoon, David. It seemed right doing it the way we did." Deeper and deeper, Gideon thought. But they would get a kick out of the true story in a couple of weeks. He hoped.

"Love at first sight?" Noah asked, disbelief in his voice.

"Why not? Seems like both of you experienced that, whether or not you *realized* it at first sight. The difference is—I did. And I realized I didn't want to wake up to another sunrise without her." He hoped his prepared line came across as sincere.

"You got married on a whim once before," Noah said in reminder.

Like he would forget that? "This isn't the same."

David came up to Gideon and looked him in the eye. "You're not telling the truth."

Gideon looked back. "About what?"

"Where's your ring?"

He slipped it out of his pocket and put it on, then held up his hand.

"Why weren't you wearing it?"

"Because I chopped wood this morning and forgot to put it back on."

"Is it engraved inside?" David asked, suspicion in his eyes.

Gideon laughed. "Is yours?"

David pulled it off and handed it to Gideon, who read it. "KISA?" Gideon asked aloud. "Did someone misspell kiss?"

"Knight in shining armor."

Gideon, trying to keep things light, put his hand on his younger brother's shoulder. "Aw. That's sweet."

David snatched back the ring and slid it on.

"No, mine's not engraved. I guess I missed that in the elopement etiquette course." Gideon wondered when it had become so easy for him to lie about being married. It shouldn't be easy.

"Why'd you stop by?" Noah asked.

"To visit. I had the afternoon free. Denise is working."

"Are you living in Sacramento with her?"

"Part of the time."

David sat on the sofa and crossed him arms, indicating he still wasn't buying Gideon's story. "Is she pregnant?"

The thought jolted Gideon. Having children was on his schedule, and both brothers knew it, but not yet. "No, David, she's not pregnant."

"I don't understand the secrecy."

"You will." He sat at the other end of the sofa. "What'd you tell Tom Anderson, Noah?"

"I told him I couldn't discuss the deal but that David and I were behind you one hundred percent, that you were a sound investment."

Gideon hadn't even known he'd needed to hear that from his brothers, needed to know they believed in him, even though he had no reason to think otherwise. They just never said things like that.

And yet he was still lying to them… .

He looked at the floor and swallowed.

After a few seconds, David put his hand on Gideon's arm and squeezed. "You didn't doubt that, did you, Gid?"

"It just feels good to hear it."

"It's the truth," Noah said. "You *are* a sound investment—personally. What I don't know is how you can afford *any* kind of deal. I know you've made a good living with your business, but it seemed like that was it."

He could give them that much truth. "I never spent a penny of the buyout you two paid me, so it kind of grew. A lot. In the beginning I didn't touch it because it was Dad's, you know? Then after it doubled and then tripled and then more, it became all mine. No taint on it anymore. But it's not enough for everything I want to do."

Noah's brows drew together. "You don't live like you have millions."

He smiled. "You're the one who taught me to be frugal."

"Okay," Noah said after everyone took a minute to let Gideon's words sink in. "Everyone is calmer. Before we go on to talk about your marriage and when we can throw you a party, why don't you give us details about this deal you're trying to swing. Maybe we can help."

He didn't want to get his hopes up that they might partner with him. He'd gotten them involved in a risky venture before that hadn't paid off—but it'd been ten years ago. This was different. This was well planned. It was still a risk, but he'd studied the whole deal from every angle, with professional input, not just his enthusiasm to guide him. He relayed all the details to his brothers, with no real expectation of them coming aboard.

The meeting ended with the promise that he would return in the morning with the investment package and the scale model. David was impulsive enough that he would probably give his answer soon, but Gideon didn't think Noah would. He was the most conservative of them about money, having a longer memory about much poorer days.

Plus Gideon worried about having his brothers involved at all. He felt as sure as he could about the venture, but nothing was guaranteed. His relationship with them was more important than any deal.

But Noah and David could very well be his last chance.

In her office, Denise hung up the phone after hearing from Gideon that none of their potential investors had called. But maybe the Bakers hadn't drummed up any interest from someone else. Maybe they would give Gideon an extension rather than have no deal on the table at all, since he wouldn't make an offer for the land only, needed to be sure of building the entire complex.

Short of asking, there wasn't any way she and Gideon could learn whether his was the only bid; therefore, they couldn't take any chances. They either got the offer in on New Year's Eve, or lose the opportunity. Maybe. *Probably*.

Denise got up from her desk and walked to a window. She'd exhausted her contacts. He had, too. And yet on the phone he hadn't seemed without hope. She liked his attitude. It was a big part of why he would be successful. Someone just needed to take a chance on him.

You. You could take a chance on him.

The words whispered in her head.

She straightened. Her legs felt rooted in place. She couldn't move, only think. The voice inside her got louder, more insistent.

You could be his partner.

She gripped the window frame, let the words settle. She was always cautious with money, without any real need to be, except that she would need some to seed each new branch of her business. But, over all, she'd rather have a lower-interest, slow-building investment than anything that might put her funds in jeopardy.

Jeopardy? Was that how she felt about his plan? No one would know it from the way she'd been trying to sell the idea. No. She believed in it. Believed in *him*. Wanted him to see his dream come true. More than anything in the—

She went rigid as the truth hit her full force—she not only believed in him, she was falling in love with him.

She brought both hands to her mouth and whispered the words into them. "I'm falling in love with him." She knew it because his dreams mattered more than her own. She'd known it from the first day. If she hadn't already been falling for him, she never would've agreed to his crazy scheme to pretend to be married.

That explained why it hadn't bothered her that Gabe and Cristina Marquez thought she'd married him. Because she'd wanted to be married to him, even then. She'd *wanted* that whole scenario he'd created about them falling in love and eloping to be true, that they'd wanted each other that badly, loved each other that much, were so sure of it.

How does someone truly know that after just a few hours?

She didn't know the answer. She only knew it was true. No, not entirely. Because the truth was even deeper now that she'd spent time with him. She loved knowing that he would be waiting when she got home from work. Couldn't wait to see him.

She swallowed as her throat started to burn. She wasn't just falling, she'd *already* fallen, head over heels, heart over reason.

Now what?

He had a plan, a schedule for himself, just as she did. He needed to get the resort up and running, then he would look toward personal success—marriage and a family.

Was it selfish of her to want him to have quick success so that he would look at her with different eyes?

That he would look beyond just the sexual attraction and onto hearth and home and forever?

She couldn't believe she was even thinking that. It would mean giving up her own dream of building her empire.

Would that be so bad?

She stared at the horizon, wishing she could see him right then, but also recognizing she needed time to keep her new, fragile revelation to herself, test it out a little. She realized why she'd been so worn down lately—she'd achieved enough of her goal and didn't need to prove anything anymore, not to anyone, not even her father. She'd built a business from the bottom up. A successful business.

But she also hadn't acknowledged her own fear until now—that her father's rejection, his firing her, had made her unsure of herself in the hotel business. Well, no more uncertainty now. Gideon needed her. She could help.

Maybe now she could have a life, too. And success in the hotel business, which would be so sweet.

And Gideon. First of all, she wanted Gideon. But whether or not she could have him, she wanted him to know how it felt to achieve his goal, as she had. She needed to make sure it happened for him. Then maybe there would be a chance for her. For them.

However, offering a partnership wouldn't be simple. He would have all sorts of objections, she was sure. How could she convince him? The biggest obstacle would be that he might feel obligated to her in some way. She didn't want him out of obligation, not personally, not professionally. She didn't want him to reject her for those very same reasons, either. How could she manage that?

A movement caught her eye as she headed back to her desk to brainstorm a plan on paper. She looked out her open door—and spotted her father in the lobby just as he spotted her.

He gave her receptionist a charming smile, said, "I see her, thank you," then walked toward her office, where he shut the door behind him.

Neither of them made a move to hug each other, even though it was still instinctive for her to reach for him. With her thumb she touched her ring finger, making sure it was empty. Sometimes she forgot. And now she wished she could wear it all the time....

"Hello, Deni."

"Hi, Dad." *What have you heard? What do you know—because you must know something or you wouldn't have come in person. How much trouble are you going to make for me? More important, for Gideon? I won't let you hurt him. I won't.*

He looked around. At sixty-one Lionel Watson had aged well, his silver hair always neatly styled, his clothing impeccable, just the right depth of tan on his face. He'd never been an ounce overweight that she could recall. He carried his success well.

"Very impressive office," he said.

"Thank you. Have a seat." She could tell he didn't like having her sit behind her desk while he took a guest chair, but she needed the protection of her desk, where she felt more in control.

He cocked his head. "I'm still always surprised to see you as a brunette."

"It took me a while, too. It's served its purpose."

"Of keeping the paparazzi away?"

"Recognition, in general." Something had shifted between them. She felt as if she were an equal now that she'd accomplished so much, earned the right to call herself successful. It made her sit up more—and yet also relax. That was a rarity for her in his presence.

"I've checked out your company," he said. "You've done very well. Made quite a name for yourself with the high-end placement business."

"I'm happy with how it's turned out. What are you doing here, Dad? Why didn't you call?"

"Calling doesn't seem to bring results," he said, his smile slight. "You've been ignoring your mother's messages, so I was dispatched. I also brought your Christmas gifts. They're being delivered to your condo right now."

Since he never did anything he didn't want to, she didn't think he'd come based on her mother's wishes. "Thanks, I mailed yours a couple of weeks ago."

"Yes, they're under the tree. Your mother would like it if you would come home for Christmas, you know."

"And you? Would you like it?" She could see it threw him off his game a little, having her question him so directly.

"Of course I would. It would be wonderful having the whole family together. Maybe go to Paris for a few days."

Paris. There was a time when that had thrilled her. "It's hard for me to be away over the holidays. Maybe when things settle down sometime in January." *Come on, Dad. Why are you here?*

"Let me know. I'll send the jet for you, so you can bypass the airport celebrity chasers." He got up and went over to a wall holding framed certificates for community projects and charity participation. "Do people leave you alone now?"

"What do you mean?"

"Are you put on the spot because of being my daughter? Because of your past?"

"I think I've earned myself a good reputation. No, I can't say it matters to anyone. Most people never make the connection. I'm almost positive I would escape notice at the airport now."

"That's how you like it, I guess."

"Yes." She went to stand beside him, deciding he wasn't going to get down to business while she kept the desk as a barrier between them. "Why are you really here?"

His smile was tight. "You're still all about business, aren't you? No idle chitchat."

She hadn't always been that way, especially not with him. She'd adored him, had trailed him like a puppy. "Not with you, I guess. We haven't 'chatted' in a very long time. So. What's going on?"

"Some news reached me."

She stopped short of heaving a huge sigh. Had he always been this dramatic? "About?"

"That you intervened in a project James Madigan was signed to, took the business elsewhere, and to a novice, at that."

Denise let out a slow, relieved breath. If he'd heard she was "married," he would've led with that. "First of all, Dad, Madigan was hired to design a hotel, not to build it."

"You know that's usually implied, especially if the design is accepted."

"Well, this time it isn't happening. His plan was uninspired and ordinary." So Madigan had told her father, but how did he know about *her* involvement in the plan? Madigan had only dealt with Gideon. "Second, the new architect is hardly a novice, not with twenty-five years of experience."

"Not in the hotel business. Not even anything remotely close to it."

They stood like duelists, the tension thick and hot between them. "She came up with an incredible design. That's all that matters." Although technically the basic design had been Denise's, Cecily had built on it.

"Did you do this because you're angry at Madigan?" Lionel asked.

"Did I do what?"

"Take away his account."

"It was a business decision," she said, parroting what he'd told her all those years ago when he'd fired her. "Nothing personal."

"You made it clear to me that you thought he wasn't competent."

"No, I said he was idiotic. And if he was so competent, why did you go ahead with the plans *I'd* created?" She'd kept her hurt locked up for so long. "Do you have any idea how insulted I was? How much pain that caused me? To have my own father fire me, then use my plans, and with *Trevor's* name attached to them? You just about destroyed me. For what?"

"I knew you would survive," he said quietly, surely. "Trevor needed it more than you. It turned out to be the right move. He's done well."

Stunned, Denise shook her head. "If that was true, why didn't you just tell me? Give me another place in the company where I could thrive? You fired me. Flat-out fired me."

"Because you always would've been the one to shine, not him. And look what you've done. You've accomplished more than he ever could on his own, but he's managed well where he is. It was the right thing to do. I'd do it again."

Denise had a decision to make. She could get angry, could kick him out and tell him she didn't want to see him again….

Or she could use the information to her advantage. To Gideon's advantage. "Did you ever take into consideration how much my life would change? My whole world? For two years I floundered. Yet even when the paparazzi started creating public havoc for me, you never said anything. Even when I got caught kissing someone else's fiancé, the most disgusting thing I ever did. Even then you never told me to quit being a brat. Never threatened to cut me off. Why not? Did you feel guilty about messing with my life?"

"Of course I did."

"Just a little, though, right? Not a whole lot."

"If I hadn't felt guilty I would've done those things you said. I figured you would reach the end of your rope with me and go do something. Accomplish something. And you did. That's who you are."

"You owe me for all that grief."

He looked amused. "Do I?"

"You do if you ever want to get things back on track with us. If you want us to be together as a family again."

He didn't roll his eyes, but his tone of voice implied the same thing. "What do you want, Deni?"

She gestured for him to sit again, and she took her place behind her desk. Oh, yes, this felt good. She was in control now. She was calm. Steady. Gideon would be proud.

"I'm going to write a check from my trust fund," she said, knowing what she had to do. She needed to give herself time for Gideon to fall in love with her, without the relationship being tied up in business. "I need you to find someone to take the money as guarantee, but sign a contract to commit that money in their own name as an investor in the project Madigan is no longer involved in. A completely hands-off investor. That point has to be made clear."

"That's all?"

"That's all."

"Then I would be forgiven? You won't hold anything else over my head? You'll come home once in a while and see your mother instead of her always coming here?"

"That's the deal. With one condition. It can't be anyone who has any interest in Watson Hotels or any company that *you* have any interest in. You can't be part of the investment except to broker it."

"I'll need a day or two to give you a name."

"You have until Saturday. That's two days." Which gave them nine more days before they had to present the offer, enough time to get contracts drawn up and signed.

"So, this Gideon Falcon is that important to you?"

"I like the deal he's trying to make."

He folded his arms. "I've kept an eye on your trust. You rarely tap into it, only to buy your condo, as far as

I know, and endow the charities you've always favored. Oh, don't look at me like that. I may not control your funds, but I'll be damned if I'd let you use up what your grandparents left you."

"Like Trevor has?" She was guessing, but she figured she was right.

"Trevor needs more guidance. And believe it or not, he's missed you."

Denise was quiet for a long time. She'd missed her brother, too, but the brother of her childhood, not the man he'd become. "Are you proud of me, Dad?"

"Without question. Although this deal you want to get yourself involved in makes me wonder. Is it this Falcon guy who's making you reckless?"

"The project is sound. It may not bring a return for a few years, but it'll be money well spent."

He met her gaze dead on. "You're in love with him."

"I have faith in him. Sometimes people need to know that."

"Point noted." He stood. "Can I take you to dinner? Both of you?"

"Another time, perhaps, Dad," she said, standing, too, and walking with him to the door. "Give Mom my love."

Then he did something that caught her off-guard, something he hadn't done in years. He hugged her. Tears burned her throat and eyes. "Thank you for coming," she said.

"I've missed you," he said gruffly, letting her go.

"Me, too. For a very long time."

She watched him walk away. Her life had taken some sudden, amazing turns today. She and her father were on the same path again. She'd found a way to help Gideon.

And she'd realized she was in love with him.

Everything had just become simple—and so much more complicated. It could all backfire, could blow up in her face.

She just didn't see any other solution.

Chapter Eleven

Gideon heard Denise's key in the lock. He looked up from the pot he was stirring as she came through the door. She stopped when she saw him, her smile brighter than usual, as if she hadn't seen him in weeks or something.

"Santa came early," he said, gesturing to the trees, under which were a whole lot of gifts that had been delivered a little while ago. He'd peeked at a few tags. They were all from her parents.

She set her briefcase and coat on the console table by the front door and came toward him, not stopping until she reached him. "Hi," she said, her cheek against his, her arms closing around him. "Dinner smells great."

If she hadn't been smiling, he would've thought the fierce hug was in reaction to something bad happening. He plunked his spoon onto the counter so that he could hold her in return. She'd hugged him spontaneously now and then, but this felt different.

"What's going on?" he asked, stroking her hair, tangling his fingers in the long, soft locks.

"My father came to see me. My mother made him."

"I can't picture anyone making your father do anything, including your mother, but I suppose stranger things have happened."

"I don't even care," she said, angling back enough to make eye contact. "We've settled things between us."

He saw relief and happiness in her eyes—no, more than that. Deep down joy. She framed his face with her hands and kissed him. He didn't hesitate to take it deeper, to slip his hands over her rear and pull her closer, keeping her body against his. She made a little sound, something between a gasp and a groan, then came at him, attacking his mouth, nipping at his lower lip, running her tongue soothingly along it, then nipping again.

"If I'd known this would be the end result, I would've gone down and settled things with your father a long time ago," he said.

She lunged at him. He moved her against the refrigerator, slid a hand down her leg to her knee and drew it up to his hip, bringing her even closer, aligning their hips, her skirt high on her thighs. He felt her garter, the top of her stocking, then the smooth skin above it. His gaze locked with hers, he slipped his hands between their bodies, unbuttoned her blouse and shoved the fabric aside, revealing a white barely-there lace bra. He could see her nipples, deep pink and hard. As he stared at her, she pulled his shirt loose.

He didn't know what to think. Where was this

leading? Why had she changed their relationship so suddenly? So drastically.

Did he really want answers?

She glided her hands along his hot, damp skin, over his abdomen, up his chest, then slowly back down. Her fingers toyed with the hair below his navel, tugging and teasing. He looked her in the eye as he cupped her breasts, closed his hands over them, felt her nipples against his palms. She had the most perfect body... .

He ran his tongue along the edge of her bra, then moved lower. He heard her groan, felt her arch toward him more, cradling his head in her arms to keep him where he was, letting him know what she wanted. But he also wanted to see her. All of her. Naked.

"Let's take this to the bedroom, Mrs. Falcon."

He'd chosen the wrong words, ones that were a reminder of their situation, their business deal, instead of his hunger for her, something that intensified every day.

Her hesitation confirmed his thoughts. He didn't give her a chance to reject him, but pulled her blouse over her.

"Probably not the best idea, after all," he said. Maybe if they were stuck living together for months or even weeks to come, they could be forgiven for giving in to their need. But they didn't have long. "Sorry," he said.

She gripped her blouse shut. Her face was flushed, her hair messy. She looked magnificent. "No apology necessary. None at all. Um, I'll be back."

When she returned later, she wore jeans and a soft, fuzzy turtleneck sweater, her hair up in a clip. On her feet were green Christmas socks, embellished with candy canes. If he hadn't known what had just happened between them, he would only wonder why her cheeks were unusually pink—and would've chalked it up to the roaring fire he'd started before she got home. Talking about it with her probably wasn't a good idea at this point.

"Can I help with dinner?" she asked as she put the teakettle on to boil.

"Soup just needs to simmer for another ten minutes or so." He gave another stir to the pot of minestrone soup, having added chicken to it to make it a full meal. "I have some bad news."

"You heard from Gabe?"

"Not yet, which surprises me. But since we talked earlier, both Anderson and Copperfield decided against coming on board. Both were apologetic. Just not the kind of deal they see working for them. Best of luck, and all that."

"Okay."

Okay? That was it? She really was in an odd mood tonight.

He glanced at the Christmas trees, now with ten packages under each of them. "I hadn't noticed how unfinished the trees looked without presents until they were there."

"Me, either."

"Want to talk about your father?" he asked. He wondered if part of her reaction was that she was embarrassed now to be with him, since they'd taken things farther than ever before, physically.

"We finally were honest with each other. He told me why he fired me. I'll tell you about it later, but for now I just need to let it sink in a little. Oh, and that he was proud of me. It was a big step for both of us."

"This was family day, I guess. I went to see my brothers." He put a foil-wrapped package of Italian bread in the oven. "The timing couldn't have been more opportune. I arrived within minutes of them finding out everything."

"Everything, as in we're supposedly married, or that they know about your deal?"

"Both."

He laughed at her expression, a cross between oops and now what?

"How did they hear?" she asked.

"It's a small world. Tom Anderson called Noah, then mentioned meeting my wife, etcetera, etcetera."

"Well, that must've been awkward. What did your brothers say about you being married to me, as it were?"

"Welcome to the family?"

Her brows drew together. "You didn't tell them the truth?"

"Not yet."

"So, what happens now?"

"We've been invited to Christmas Eve at Noah's."

She stopped in her tracks, her mouth dropping open slightly. "I'm guessing the whole family will be there."

"At least. Half of Chance City could show up, for all I know."

She got a mug from the cabinet and a teabag from a canister. He could tell she was mentally sorting the information.

"I'm fine with your telling them the truth, Gideon," she said after a while. "I'm not comfortable with letting them all think we're married, then turning around and saying it was a lie, especially with the entire family, kids and all."

"At this point I think we should play it by ear. My brothers want to see the investment packet tomorrow."

She turned around instantly, frowning. "I thought they didn't want to be included."

"So they've said in the past. Plus *I've* been hesitant to include them because I'd like to have a partnership with someone not related to me. Things tend to stay less volatile if there's no history involved. Anyway, who knows what's going to happen. The Bakers might change their mind and extend the deadline again if they don't get whatever magic number they're looking for from any other bidders. Hell, at the rate it's going, we won't even have an offer to make."

"We will."

"I wish I had your confidence." He was also tired of getting his hopes up. He'd lived on the edge for a long time, years really. He was ready to step back from it and take a deep breath. If only Max hadn't died... .

The phone rang. He watched Denise look at the Caller ID box, saw her hesitate, then right before it would have gone to the answering machine, she picked it up, whispering to Gideon that she'd be back in a minute. Then she went into her bedroom and shut the door.

It was the first time she'd taken a call in private, capping off an already strange evening.

And when she came out later, she didn't say who had called.

There'd been a definite shift in their relationship today. Some he'd liked, but others? He couldn't wait for New Year's Eve to come and go.

An hour after Denise went to bed, she still tossed and turned. Not because of the visit from her father, or the phone call from her mother, who'd been giddy that Denise and her father had made up. No, she couldn't sleep because she wanted to be in Gideon's bed, making love with him, telling him she loved him, making him happy by saying she would provide the remaining funds.

She couldn't do any of it. Yet.

Loving him complicated everything.

She pushed herself up in bed and leaned against the plush, velvet headboard. She'd come to love living with him. Her social life had been fine until he came along, a series of dinners out or in, evenings of renting movies or going to movies or a play. Ways to pass time. She'd dated plenty. She'd never met anyone she would've lied for—until Gideon.

It'd seemed harmless enough at the beginning. He'd needed someone to help him look like a good risk. As she'd told her father, Gideon's project was sound, and that was the truth. She'd seen it right away. But now people thought they were married, not just business acquaintances but her friends, and his brothers, who felt left out at not being invited to the wedding.

She shoved her hair back from her face. It'd all gotten way too complicated.

But it would end. Sooner than she wanted, even, in some ways. She wished he would tell his brothers the truth, though. Lying to them seemed the worst. She didn't want anything to happen between the brothers that might hurt the sibling relationship.

Like with Trevor, she thought. She hadn't even seen her brother for five years.

Denise climbed out of bed and slipped into a robe. She went in search of a box tucked into her closet, dragged it out, then maneuvered it up onto her bed. It took her a while to peel off all the tape. Then she sat cross-legged, the box in front of her.

She removed her past from it, one item at a time, mostly photo albums and scrapbooks, but a few mementos, too. Programs from various events. Letters. Birthday cards, including a goofy one from Trevor on her tenth birthday, when he was nine. He'd made it himself, had cut out a picture of a trophy from a magazine to glue on the front, then inside, "World's Weirdest Sister." Then, "But I love you anyway. Somebody has to."

She smiled, her eyes blurry, then sifted through the rest of the cards, all store-bought after that, but with notes scribbled in them that were personal and reflecting the moment. She and Trevor had talked countless times about her running the company when their father retired. Her brother had always seemed okay with it, ribbing her about having to report to their dad, and how he would be an even more strict boss than he was a father.

Denise had escaped that fate, didn't even have a boss. She ruled her own universe, not reporting to anyone. Who'd gotten the better deal? Looking at it that way, she had to admit she—

A light knock came at her door. She tightened the sash on her robe and told Gideon to come in.

He wore blue jeans, zipped but unbuttoned. His hair was temptingly messy. He leaned against the doorjamb and crossed his arms. "Can't sleep?"

She shook her head. Her mouth had gone dry at the sight of him.

"What's in the box?" he asked.

"My past."

"Can I see?"

"Sure." She shifted everything to one side, making space for him, then set an album in his hands, the first, chronologically. Her baby book.

She could barely keep her hands off him as he hunched beside her, flipping the pages, commenting on her mother's notes about her first word—Dada; first steps—at ten months; first immunizations—she didn't make a peep but looked accusingly at the nurse. He laughed at that. Then he found a lock of her hair, so blond it was almost white.

He took her hand and put it over her newborn hand-print. If they had a baby...

Denise let herself fantasize about that for a minute. She'd bet anything that Gideon would be the kind of dad to get up during the night and bring the baby to bed to nurse. He'd change diapers, too. And walk and rock to soothe a crying infant. Some things she didn't even have to guess about. He wanted to be as different from his own father as possible. Gideon would be hands-on and openly loving.

She remembered her impression of him at the very beginning that he was edgy and a little dangerous. Maybe he was—with other people. With his family, he would be strong but gentle, as he was with her.

She wanted him to father her children.

Denise snapped to attention as Gideon waved a hand in front of her face.

"Did you fall asleep?" he asked.

"I drifted a little."

"Feeling better? Think you can sleep now?"

She nodded, and he started packing everything into the box. He held out one framed photo. "This is my favorite. What are you, a princess?"

She took it from him and ran her hand across the glass. "A bride."

"How old were you?"

"I'm missing my front teeth, so six, I guess. I made my father walk me down an aisle and give me away."

"Who was the groom?"

She laughed when she remembered. "My dog, Toby. I even put a bow tie around his neck."

He set the box on the floor, then sat beside her again. "Do you want to talk about what happened with your father today?"

"I'm not sure how I'm feeling. I'm happy, of course, but I don't completely trust him." Yet she'd asked him to make the deal for her? She was having second thoughts about that now. "That will take some time."

"Is that why you were so quiet tonight?"

"That's some of it." *I love you.* "The lies are starting to get to me."

"Yeah." He ran a hand down her hair. "I'll see you in the morning."

She wanted him to stay with her, until she fell asleep. Better yet, until morning. "I'm sorry I woke you up."

"You didn't." With that enigmatic response he left, not even looking back.

She closed her eyes and settled under the blankets, tired enough to sleep, although feeling more as if she'd just gone through the calm before a treacherous storm.

Chapter Twelve

"Gabe Marquez doesn't strike me as a man who shows up in person if the news is negative," Denise said two days later, just after noon. She lit a cinnamon candle as she talked. "We haven't heard a peep from him for six days, and he wants to meet here, rather than us going to him? I don't get it."

"I don't, either," Gideon said, enjoying her being so revved up, especially since this was the first day of four she was taking off for Christmas. Gabe had called early that morning to say he wanted to stop by. Denise had been in a frenzy ever since. "You're not wearing your ring."

She held her hand in front of her and groaned, then rushed toward her bedroom. He'd never seen her so worked up about anything. He liked it, actually, particularly after she'd been in such an odd mood the past couple of days, quiet and contemplative but in a serene everything-will-be-okay kind of way.

She refused to allow him to worry about the deadline, would change the subject every time it came up, even though they were down to two possibilities—his brothers and Gabe—with only nine days to go. Maybe only his brothers. They would know soon. Gabe should arrive any minute.

The bell rang. Gideon opened the door to find not Gabe there, but a stranger—tall, slender, his hair golden blond, his dark green eyes shifting to look at the door number in confusion.

"You must be Trevor," Gideon said, just as Denise emerged, her expression going from welcoming to shocked to joy.

"Trev!"

"Hey, sis." He grinned. "Long time."

The grin hid a lot, Gideon decided, because Trevor pushed his face against his sister's shoulder when they hugged, his grip on her visibly tight. Neither of them let go. Denise shook, as if she were crying silently, a guess confirmed when they finally pulled apart. She swiped her fingers along her cheeks and laughed shakily. Trevor's expression turned soft. He took her hand, then dropped his gaze, staring intently.

"What's this? You're married?" He shot a look at Gideon, who waited for Denise to decide how to handle it.

"This is Gideon Falcon," she said, reaching for him.

Gideon moved beside her, slid his arm around her waist and offered his hand and a greeting to her brother.

Trevor shifted a large envelope from one hand to the other. "Also wearing a wedding band," he observed as they shook hands. "When did that happen?"

She hesitated a beat. "Not long ago."

"Dad didn't mention it."

"Dad doesn't know."

Trevor looked at her, then at Gideon but said nothing. He held the envelope toward her. "Speaking of the devil…"

Her cheeks flushed. "Thanks. So he asked you to be a messenger?"

"Ordered me."

Gideon felt her go stiff.

"I'm sorry," she said, defensive.

"I was glad, Deni. I don't know why I thought I needed an invitation to come. Or an order." He started wandering around her condo, taking in everything. "If you'd lined up five houses all decorated differently, this is the last one I would've said was yours."

"Why's that?"

"Too contemporary. You always liked plush. Shabby chic."

"People change."

He gave her a long look. "Yes, they do." He studied an angel ornament on the tall tree. "Not going to offer me anything to drink after my long, grueling trip?"

"Right. An hour on the corporate jet, fully stocked with almost every beverage known to mankind." She smiled, taking the sting out of the words and headed toward the kitchen, setting the envelope on the counter.

"They were out of Cristal."

She laughed. "Us, too. But we've got beer."

"That works. I feel a toast coming on," he said, including Gideon.

She didn't question what was in the envelope, which made Gideon figure she already knew. What was going on? And why did it seem secretive?

The doorbell rang again. Gideon caught Denise's startled expression and almost laughed. When had their lives turned into a farce worthy of a theatrical production? Comings and goings, lies and truths, coincidences and misunderstandings—they only needed a slamming door or two and a scantily dressed maid.

"One of us could use the library downstairs," she said to Gideon just before he opened the door.

A flurry of greetings, introductions and apologies followed, then Gideon took Gabe out of the building to a nearby diner, encouraged by the fact Gabe had brought a briefcase with him.

Actions usually did speak louder than words.

Denise handed Trevor a bottle of beer then sat at the other end of the sofa from him. She could hardly believe he was there. The years melted away. He looked like a man now, had a man's body and face, more mature and strong.

"So. Married, huh?" he asked. "Why are you keeping it a secret?"

"Just our choice for the moment."

"Are you pregnant?"

She laughed. She could only imagine Gideon's horror. Babies weren't on his schedule for a few more years. "No. How about you? Someone special in your life?"

"Not ready to settle down." He took a long sip, contemplating her. "Dad says you're pretty successful."

"I worked hard for it. It feels really good."

"I'm sorry for the way everything turned out, you know, with Dad and the job. You got a rotten deal."

She considered how her father believed Trevor needed the job more than she had. She'd been thinking about it ever since and had decided he was right. "Over and done," she said to her brother now. She really did want to put the past behind. "Do you know what's in the envelope you brought?"

"Nope."

"Trev? Can I trust Dad?"

"About what?"

"To be true to his word. After all that happened before, and years of things being complicated between us, would he lead me to think everything was good again if it wasn't?"

"That's a little too vague for me to answer. Would he lie to you? I doubt it, not a complete lie, anyway. He might phrase something in a way he would have an out later. Would he tell you one thing and do another if it served his purpose better? I'd say yes, if it had to do with business. But with you? I don't think so, but don't hold me to it."

"Well, that's concrete and clear."

He laughed. "Dad's indefinable."

She nodded.

Trevor leaned his arms on his thighs and pierced her with a surprisingly serious look. "Do you know how hurt Mom is going to be that you got married without her?"

Guilt wrapped around Denise, creating a cocoon, hot, tight and uncomfortable. "I never wanted a big wedding or the hoopla."

"Since when? You played wedding all the time when we were kids." When she didn't reply, he said, "You're right that people change, Deni, but that doesn't mean you get married without your family there."

She wanted to tell him, ached to tell him, but if Gideon could keep the truth from his brothers for another few days, she could do the same with hers.

"There are reasons," she said. "I'll explain it all. Just not yet. Trev, I've really missed you." She was torn between wanting him to leave before she spilled her guts to him and wanting him to stay so they could catch up on everything.

He took the decision out of her hands. "I'm sorry to have to take off so fast, but I'm due in Seattle later today."

"Business or personal?"

"Business."

"Are you happy, Trev? Dad said you were doing well."

"Did he?" His mouth went tight for a few seconds. "He hasn't told me that. Not surprising, huh?"

"Not really." She always gave praise freely, knowing it made a difference in how people felt about themselves and their jobs. She'd been there herself.

"Yeah, I like what I'm doing, more than I thought I would, actually. You not being there to bail me out sorta forced me, you know?"

"Did I do that? Bail you out?"

He laughed, exasperation in his tone. "You're kidding, right? Me. Dani. Everyone. You're the champion bailer."

His comments stung. "I've always been a nurturer."

"There's a fine line between nurturing and controlling, you know? You always needed to be the one in charge. You figured less could go wrong that way."

He was right. Totally, completely, absolutely right. And here she was, doing it again. The eye-opening thought threw her off track, off the straight course she'd been on since she'd seen her father.

Trevor took his empty bottle over to the counter, setting it next to the envelope, which he patted. "Be careful, okay? Trust your instincts about whatever this deal is. Read it with a fine-tooth comb and objective eye."

"I will, thanks." She walked with him to the door. "You don't know how much it means to me, having you come."

They hugged each other, this time not so frantically. "I'll be back. Dad says you're coming down for a visit, too."

"Yes, soon."

"Don't wait too long to tell Mom your news."

"I won't." Soon there would be nothing to tell her. "Bye."

Trevor tugged on her hair and grinned. "I guess your gentleman doesn't prefer blondes," he teased, then he was gone.

She didn't hesitate but picked up the envelope and took it into her bedroom to study the documents inside. She'd asked her father to give her a name. He'd done that and more. He'd provided an entire contract.

Trust your instincts.

She'd barely gotten three pages into it when she heard the front door open. She hurried out to greet Gideon.

He shoved his hands in his pockets, his expression serious. He looked around.

"Trevor's gone. Well?" she asked, anxious.

"Gabe's in." He rushed toward her, picked her up and swung her around. "He's in."

Her eyes burned, then welled at the instant whirl of emotions. She hadn't realized how much she'd wanted to be his partner, had been counting on it.

"You're crying," he said, brushing his thumbs under her eyes.

"I'm happy for you."

"For us. Gabe flat out said that you were the key ingredient."

"Why?"

"Because you built your own business, and you know the hospitality field."

She pulled back. "You had much more to do with it than I did."

He shrugged. "Does it matter? It's going to happen."

"What kind of deal did you make?"

"Fifty-fifty. He wouldn't do anything less, but he doesn't plan to micromanage. He made a few adjustments to the contract. I didn't sign it yet."

"Good. You need to run it by your lawyer first." She didn't know what to do, how to act. Her purpose for pretending to be his wife, for having him live with her, was gone now. He would go back to his cabin. She would go back to work.

"I also didn't sign it," he added, "because I haven't gotten an answer from Noah and David yet. I need to at least hear what they have to say."

"You mean you'd be open to another offer at this point?"

"Why not? This will be a long-term partnership. Gabe's great—he's smart and innovative, and I believe him when he says he'll be hands-off unless he thinks it's necessary to involve himself. David and Noah would be different kinds of partners, probably hands-on. Probably always sticking their nose in my affairs. But they're good businessmen. Plus I only have to sway one of them, since they would each own twenty-five percent. Unless they decide to partner as one block, instead of two. That would make problems for me."

"You've thought all this through."

"I had to. I'll give my brothers time to make a decision before I accept Gabe's offer. We've got a week."

"And Gabe is willing to wait? He isn't annoyed at being put off?"

"He didn't seem to be. He understood the appeal of working with my brothers."

Denise didn't know what to do now. Should she tell him about the deal she'd arranged? Or should she just let it go, let him build his business, and hope he would want the personal side of their relationship to continue.

"Do you still need me to spend Christmas Eve with you and your family?" She didn't know what she wanted his answer to be, since *yes* meant a continuation of the lies, and *no* meant she wouldn't be with him. Past Christmases had been quietly busy but also lonely. This year would be excruciating without him.

"I'd like you there, if you don't mind," he said. "Maybe you'd rather go home now that things are settled with your family."

"I'm happy staying here with you. What if David and Noah tell you yes, Gideon? Will you accept it, knowing they would be hands-on, unlike Gabe?"

"Honestly, I don't think I'm going to know how I feel until I hear it. I'm trying to keep an open mind."

So, would there be room for a third choice of a

partner? "What if they tell you no? Will that hurt your relationship with them?"

"I would probably feel a small sting that they didn't have enough faith in me, but it wouldn't last long. They have families to support, and their pockets aren't as deep as Gabe's. But knowing I have a choice would be great, especially after all the worrying ever since Max died. I can sleep easy tonight."

"Good."

"How about you? How'd it feel to see your brother?"

"Amazing. He's really matured."

Gideon headed toward the kitchen. "I'm going to fix a sandwich. Want one?"

"Sure. I'll help."

"I can manage." He glanced back at her. "What did you tell him about us?"

"Nothing. You're keeping it secret from your brothers, so I'm doing the same." She pulled up a bar stool and sat as he pulled out sandwich fixings. She wondered if he would go back to his cabin now. There was no reason for him to stay.

It had been hard keeping her hands off him since she'd realized she was in love with him.

"You're very quiet," he said as he sliced a tomato.

"Things have been a little overwhelming, don't you think?"

"Would you like me to go home? Give you some time to yourself?"

She waited for him to make eye contact, then said, "No."

"You sure? Looks like you've got some business to attend to. The envelope your brother brought."

She knew he was waiting for her to tell him about it. She hadn't decided what to do yet. "I need to read through what he brought, but that's all."

He set the knife down. "We made a deal, Denise. We both said we'd be honest and not make each other guess."

"I'll tell you about it. Just not right now." She went into the kitchen to get them both something to drink. "I don't want you to go, Gideon, but I'd understand if you'd like to be in your own home again."

After another minute he set their plates on the counter. "Yeah, I think I'd like to be home. I'm going to help with the Christmas Eve dinner. I can do some things ahead of time. You're welcome to come along."

She couldn't gauge from his tone whether he really wanted her to or was being polite, since he knew she wouldn't go into the office until the day after Christmas, four days from now. "You don't have a guest room."

"The couch is comfortable. I can sleep there."

The tone of the whole day had changed drastically. They should've been celebrating. Instead they were tip-toeing around each other. Maybe they did need a break from each other.

"I need to show my face at Cecily's party tonight," she said, "which you weren't crazy about attending, and then there's Sunday brunch with Stacy tomorrow morning that you weren't going to, anyway. Maybe I could come up early Christmas Eve day and help with the food."

"That's fine." He turned away, carrying his utensils to the sink to rinse. "Or come tomorrow after brunch, if you want."

"I'll give you a call when I get home. We can decide then."

"Okay."

They ate their meal in silence. Denise didn't understand it. Now that he had an investor lined up, he wouldn't need her anymore, but she hadn't expected him to just back away so easily.

He went to pack while she did the dishes, then she walked to the front door with him.

"See you in a couple of days—or tomorrow," he said, not setting down his luggage, apparently not intending to hug her goodbye.

"Let me know if your brothers give you an answer, okay?"

"Of course. Then you wouldn't have to come at all, I guess. You could even go home. I'm sure your father would send the jet for you."

She hesitated. "Are you angry at me?"

His jaw twitched. "Honestly, I don't know what I'm feeling, except that I know you're keeping something from me. We made a deal not to have secrets."

"I promise I'll explain it." She touched his arm. "I'm really happy for you, Gideon."

After a tight, tense moment, he dropped his bag and hauled her to him. His kiss may have lacked the finesse of the other times, the gentleness, but it said a lot more to her. Here was the dangerous, edgy man she'd seen before, the one who appealed to her orderly life, who promised a walk on the wild side. And he wanted her.

When he finally released her, he ran his fingers across her tender lips. She waited for him to change his mind about leaving. She'd already told him she didn't want him to go. All he had to do was not walk out the door.

"Thank you," he said, low and harsh, then he left.

Denise stared at the closed door. He'd lived with her for a week. Only a week. Yet his leaving felt like a divorce, as if he'd had the option of trying to make the relationship work but decided not to.

How much more devastating was it going to be when the real end came?

Chapter Thirteen

Two days later Gideon was contemplating the Denise situation, as he'd begun calling it, amid five kids helping him make appetizers. For a man who wanted to step back from the edge, he sure was doing a lot of leaning out over the canyon of the unknown.

At the moment, he was waiting for Denise to arrive for the Christmas Eve festivities. The kids were a distraction from the anticipation as they crowded around the center island in Noah's kitchen, covered with trays and bowls. So far the children had been working in harmony, but it couldn't last much longer. A couple of the natives were already restless.

But then, so was he. He hadn't seen Denise for two days, had talked to her twice—tense, brief conversations—but that was it.

Which was why he'd told her to meet him at Noah's

instead of at his cabin. Everyone here thought they were married. It would be expected that he give her a greeting worthy of newlyweds who hadn't seen each other for a couple of days. They would have to be physically close, to talk, to smile. Act as if they'd missed each other.

It wouldn't be an act for him. He'd missed her much more than he'd anticipated, starting from the moment he'd gotten into his car at her place. He'd kicked himself the whole drive home for not staying on with her, especially since she'd wanted him to.

He might have, too, except for the fact she was keeping something from him.

"Adam, you're squishing that tomato to death," came a strident female voice.

"So? It's just gonna get squished in someone's mouth, anyways, Ashley Perfect."

The manner in which his nieces and nephews were stuffing mushrooms and cherry tomatoes was almost predictable. Those who were by nature fidgety didn't like the tedious process of preparing tiny hors d'oeuvres. The more patient ones were doing the best, most efficient work.

"They're supposed to look pretty, aren't they, Uncle Gideon?" Ashley asked.

"That's the goal, yes. Adam, why don't you open the box of crackers and start filling that tray with them. Neatly. Spread them out so that the edges touch but don't lap over each other."

"All right!" The nine-year-old hopped down, grabbed the box, then pretended to make a dunk shot with it on his way back to the island. "I don't know why we hafta do this girl stuff, anyways."

"Excuse me?" Gideon said, holding his arms out.

"Well, not counting you. Everyone knows the good cooks are men. Women do the grunt work."

Gideon grabbed Ashley's arm in time to stop her from throwing a handful of bread crumbs at her brother.

"Time out," came a voice from behind him, the soon-to-be-stepmother, Tricia, another of Denise's perfect employee placements. "Sugar cookies are on the dining room table. Frosting and candies are all set out. Go wild."

The kids hopped down from their stools and shoved their way into the dining room. Noah's twelve-year-old twins Ashley and Zoe, his nine-year-old twins Adam and Zach, and David's almost-adopted eight-year-old daughter, Hannah, cheered as they went.

"You sent my help away," Gideon griped to Tricia, a tall, blond woman possessed with great patience and a sense of humor.

"Two more minutes and you would've had a mutiny on your hands. You can thank me anytime now."

"Thanks." He meant it, too. He'd seen what was about to happen. "Getting five kids to sit still on Christmas Eve was probably a bad idea. I appreciate your pitching in."

She smiled and stuffed filling into a tomato. "This is the extent of my culinary skills, by the way, so don't give me any other assignment. I'm sure Valerie will create something phenomenal, like Yorkshire pudding or something."

He laughed. Valerie and Tricia were like night and day, yet each one perfect for her particular Falcon man. "I don't think so. Not for a buffet."

She shrugged. "So, I hear congratulations are in order. You're a sly pair."

"I would say more like impulsive."

"Denise doesn't strike me as the impulsive type, and I don't know you well enough to say whether that's true of you—except that I heard you got married once before sort of on a whim, and it didn't last long."

He'd been counting on people remembering his previous marriage and the similarities to this one, so that he could just have everyone shrug and say, "Well, that's Gideon for you." Except that he didn't view his relationship with Denise in anywhere near the same way.

"I tend to make quick decisions," he said. "They can't all be winners."

Her eyes sparkled. "True. Although it sounds like you took your time with this Trails project you discussed with Noah."

"Yeah. A lifetime."

A car came down the driveway. "Noah's home," Tricia said, grabbing a hand towel, then hurrying out to greet him, joy in her expression.

Gideon envied his brother. Denise had been happy to see him every night, too. He knew how good it felt to have someone waiting for you—or coming home to you.

He glanced out the window when he heard another car approach. Denise, right on time. He was surprised at how his stomach tightened. Unsure of the reason, he took his time, washing his hands before going outside, amazed at his nerves, the anticipation of seeing her again.

She stood talking with Noah and Tricia, but she turned toward him as he made his way.

He couldn't see her expression, only her body language. She pulled a red-shot-with-gold shawl a little closer over a decently indecent red dress, the illusion of sexiness without displaying much skin, and as a result *incredibly* sexy. Glittery gems decorated her throat and wrist—and her ring finger. Tall, red high heels showed off those gorgeous long legs.

He'd never seen a sexier woman in his life. Especially when she smiled at him as he came up to her. He took her into his arms and kissed her, heard Noah mutter something about impressionable children before he and Tricia walked off.

She tasted like Christmas. "Hello, Mrs. Falcon." He used the term deliberately, a reminder of how others saw them but also just to say it out loud.

"Mountain man." She combed his hair with her fingers, the image of a loving, devoted wife. "Anything in particular I should know for tonight?"

"Like?"

"Have they given you an answer yet?"

"No." He slipped an arm around her waist and headed toward the house.

"Should I bring it up? Not bring it up?"

"I trust your judgment, Denise. I won't censure you."

She looked at him with appreciation. Of the three Falcon brothers, Gideon figured he was probably the least into traditional roles for men and women, always had been, although he certainly enjoyed the differences between the sexes.

"Is it your preference that I don't bring it up?" she asked.

"It's Christmas Eve."

She smiled. "Got it." She hooked a thumb behind her. "I brought a change of clothes, in case I needed to dress down to help."

"There's not a whole lot left to do. I cooked quite a bit, and Valerie's bringing most of the rest. We're almost done fixing the appetizers. We're casual."

She stopped. "Casual? Why didn't you tell me? I'm overdressed, aren't I?" She smothered a groan. "I'm going to look ridiculous."

"You look beautiful."

She closed her eyes for a few seconds, then looked straight at him. "I can't do anything right. These lies are wearing me down, Gideon. I'm having a very hard time facing your family knowing we aren't married but acting like we are."

"Well, we could hop in the car, drive to Reno and do it," he suggested, trying to get her to lighten up, not showing how much the lies had gotten to him, too, especially with his brothers. He honestly had never expected them to find out. "But then there would be the issue of a real divorce instead of a fake one. And we wouldn't have time for a prenup, which I'm sure you agree would be a necessity."

She looked down. "Of course."

"So there's nothing we can do to change our situation, right? It'll be over soon. For now, let's just enjoy ourselves."

A car turned into the driveway and beeped. "Here's David and Valerie. Relax, okay? Everything's going to be fine. Feel free to act wifely."

She laughed, low and shaky, relief in her eyes. "So I get to be right all the time?"

He grinned. "Have at it. And look over there. Valerie's all dressed up, too. Feel better?"

She nodded.

He realized he wouldn't like her anywhere near as much if her conscience hadn't been bothering her. But it also made him wonder about the secret she was keeping from him. Wasn't her conscience eating at her about that, too?

David had parked the car next to the back door, close to the kitchen. If he and Noah had made a decision yet, Gideon couldn't read it in David's face. He just looked happy. Happier than he'd ever been. And the reason for it had gotten out of the car on the other side and run right to Denise to hug her.

"We can always celebrate our anniversaries together," Valerie said. "Won't that be fun!"

"Four's a crowd on a wedding anniversary, don't you think?" David asked dryly as he opened the tailgate, revealing a couple of boxes of foil-wrapped dishes.

Valerie hugged Gideon. "I was so shocked when David told me your news, but also so pleased for you both. We'll talk about the details of your reception later, okay? You *are* going to let us do that for you, right? Unless your parents plan to? I don't even know where they live."

When Denise didn't say anything, Gideon chimed in. "Let's get through the holidays first. Starting with now. Everything smells great," he said as he hefted a box. "Tamales?"

"Good nose," Valerie said.

"She spent days getting ready for this," David said, his own arms loaded as he headed to the back door.

"It made me happy." Valerie linked arms with Denise. "I've never had a big family. It was just my mom and me forever, then just Hannah and me, after she was born. I had a wonderful time this week. I love this family so much. Especially my knight in shining armor." She flashed a brilliant, loving smile toward David. "And now you're part of it, Denise. What a merry Christmas this will be for all of us, our first together as a family."

Gideon didn't look at Denise. He didn't want to see whatever she was feeling—or trying to hide.

He should regret having gotten her involved—and he did regret that she had to lie for him—but otherwise, he had no regrets at all.

"I have been waiting all night," Tricia said in a rush to Denise as the three women finished up in the kitchen after dinner. Everyone had pitched in, creating a fascinating hive of activity, people moving around each other in a strange dance, conversation and laughter filling the space. "Spill, girlfriend."

Denise had been avoiding being alone with Tricia and Valerie. They'd become good friends in a short period of time, not just because Denise had placed them in jobs with David and Noah, but because of Valerie's bachelorette party, where they'd all let down their hair.

"I think you know the details," Denise said, as evasive as possible.

"We know you eloped. But why didn't you announce it?" Valerie asked.

"We just wanted to keep it to ourselves for a while. What about you, Tricia?" Denise asked, changing the subject. "Have you and Noah set a date?"

"We're talking about Valentine's Day. He figures he couldn't forget our anniversary that way." She grinned.

"That's perfect," Valerie said, untying her apron, looking satisfied that the kitchen was in order. "Gives us time to organize a party for Gideon and Denise, too."

"That's very thoughtful," Denise said, wishing she had more dishes to do, or leftovers to wrap, anything to keep her occupied.

"Yeah, yeah, yeah," Tricia said. "Quit being so evasive. We want to hear about how you fell in love so fast. What is it about these Falcon men, anyway? They're just so lovable! I know you met Gideon at the bachelorette party. You never said a word at the wedding about it, and you must've gotten together during that week. All I saw was how you danced the night away, only with each other."

Denise decided they weren't going to give up, so she offered the story that Gideon had concocted, the one that had sold her on the idea. "It's short and sweet and…magical. We danced and talked and touched, and then we just knew, in a flash of recognition, we absolutely knew that we were soul mates. Were we crazy to run off like that? Probably. But there wasn't another solution for us."

"Do you regret it?" Valerie asked. "I mean not having your family there, not having the fancy ceremony and all that?"

Yes. She wanted to scream the word. Trevor was right. She'd always wanted a fairy-tale wedding. It didn't have to be huge, but it needed a beautiful gown and her father giving her away and her mother crying. She wanted the first corny dance, the first bite of sugary cake and the silly champagne toast.

She wanted the honeymoon....

With Gideon. She'd watched him all evening, as a brother, a brother-in-law and an uncle. She'd seen how the children adored him and confirmed what a great father he would make. She'd watched all of them mix and mingle, and she'd suddenly craved that for herself. She wanted her own family.

"Yes, a little," she said finally, in response to Valerie's question, aware that both women were waiting silently, patiently for her to respond. "But regret isn't something I lug around with me. Does no good, anyway."

"Amen, sister," Tricia said.

Adam raced into the kitchen, taking the corner at full speed, his sneakers squealing as he came to a quick stop. "We're going to open presents. Hurry up!"

Denise sought out Gideon in the living room. He was leaning against the fireplace mantel, a Christmas toddy in his hand, laughing at something David was saying. Gideon locked gazes with her. The smile left his face, replaced with an intense, hungry look that matched how she felt. She moved into his arms to hold and be held.

"Too mushy, Uncle Gideon," Adam announced, his twin, Zach, dittoing it.

"Someday you won't think that," Gideon said to them, a smile forming, then he kissed her, a light, tender caress, making her crave more.

"Having fun?" he asked.

"Yes."

"Good."

She turned around to face the crowd, leaning against him, his arms around her waist, as colorful packages were handed around and oohed and aahed over.

After a fun-filled hour, the festivities wrapped up. Denise was in the kitchen with Valerie, who was sorting packages of leftovers to send home with them so that they wouldn't have to cook the next day.

Was that even an issue? He hadn't invited her to stay with him, but she'd packed a bag, just in case. And everything had been easy with him all evening, not the strained conversation she'd worried about, given the way they'd left each other the last time, and their brief talks since.

Still, she couldn't presume that she would stay over at his place. Except he had volunteered once before to sleep on his couch, after all.

He came into the kitchen, his gifts almost overflowing from a shopping bag. His expression... She didn't even know how to describe it. He looked like a kid who'd just seen Santa for himself and now believed.

A minute later they were walking toward her car, only the sound of her footfalls reaching them. His registered no noise. How did he do that? She often forgot what he did for a living, how adventurous he was, how skilled he must be. She'd like to see him in action.

"Come home with me," he said into the quiet when they reached her car.

She didn't even debate. Her pulse went into instant overdrive. "Okay. I'll follow you."

"Keep up."

She laughed. "Don't lose me."

He framed her face with his hands and kissed her. Then he got into his car and led the way home.

Chapter Fourteen

Fifteen minutes later Denise turned off her engine and pressed the trunk release. By the time she'd gathered up her purse and shawl and walked to the rear, Gideon was pulling her overnight bag out of the trunk.

"You came prepared," he said, no inflection whatsoever in his voice.

"I didn't want to risk getting snowed in without my essentials."

He shut the trunk and picked up his bag of gifts and a smaller one with the leftovers. "Interesting. I didn't hear any predictions of snow."

"Really? I'm positive I heard that," she said lightly.

"I think you're snowing me."

She laughed, grabbed his gift bag to lighten his load and headed to the house.

"Take my arm, please," he said. "I don't know why

you insist on wearing those stilts, but it's a treacherous thing to do here at night."

"You *do* know why." She tucked her hand under his arm, happy to comply.

"Because they make you feel sexy."

She nodded. More important, *he* made her feel sexy.

"Which means that under that silky dress, you're wearing some interesting lingerie again. For the same reason."

"No problem with your memory, obviously." They climbed the stairs. A motion detector set off a spotlight to guide them.

Inside the house, Gideon went straight to the fireplace. Denise saw that it was ready to light. He only had to set a match to it. Something he always did? Or hopeful that she would come home with him? She couldn't remember from the other time she'd been there.

She took the leftovers into the kitchen and stored them. "Can I fix you anything to eat or drink?" she called out.

No answer.

"Gideon?"

Still no answer.

She straightened and shut the door, then jumped back. He was standing there on quiet feet again, holding a thin box wrapped in Christmas paper. She thought about the wrapped one she had, too, in her suitcase.

"Go ahead," he said, holding it out. "Open it."

The lid was wrapped separately, so all she had to do was lift it. Under layers of tissue paper she found more paper. A document. A legal document.

"David and Noah gave me that right before we left

the house," he said. "They're in. They're making themselves one fifty-percent block instead of two twenty-five percent blocks, but they're in."

"Oh, Gideon! That's wonderful." She reached for him and hugged him hard, blinking back the tears that threatened. She couldn't give him her gift now. "I'm happy for you. So happy. Did you accept them?"

He moved away, putting the lid back on the box, his hands unsteady. "No."

"Why not?"

"I need to think about it. Whether I want to involve them. As we talked about before, there are advantages and disadvantages."

"When will you decide?"

"I don't know. Soon. I just need to give it some thought. It means a lot that they believe in my project. A lot." He gave her a quirky smile. "Again, you were the tipping point."

"In what way?"

"They said the same things as Gabe Marquez."

"What? That I'd built my own business and know the hospitality field? Seriously?"

He moved his shoulders. "They may have also added something about you being steady and good for me. That kind of thing."

"They really don't know you, do they?" she asked, confused. "You don't need me for your success. You only needed a partner for the money angle, not because you can't run the show yourself."

"Thank you, but you see me as I am now. Siblings have long memories." He grinned. "Does it matter? It's not just a dream anymore. Two weeks ago I'd thought it would never happen. Now I even have a choice. Maybe."

"Maybe?"

"The Bakers still have to accept my offer. I wish there was a way to know if they have anyone else interested, although I guess it wouldn't change much for me. I can't go back to Gabe or my brothers and ask for more money."

Maybe she should tell him now....

"But there's time enough to worry about that. Tonight, no more talk about business."

Which meant they were avoiding the elephant in the room—that now that he was assured of a partner, he needed nothing more from her. Except a "divorce."

"You're very quiet," he said. "Are you tired?"

"Recovering from the noise and activity. I'm not used to it."

"But you had a good time?" He took her hand and guided her to the couch as the fire caught hold and flared.

"I had a great time. Our Christmases were more... sedate than yours. Fun, but quiet. Very often we went to Paris or London. How about you?"

"I can't say my father was into the whole Christmas thing, but David's mother, who was with us the longest, did her best."

"There's always so much expectation, isn't there? So many ways we can be disappointed after all the hype."

He put his arm around her and pulled her close. She laid her head on his shoulder and watched the fire, enjoying the strength and heat of his body.

"This Christmas hasn't been a disappointment," he said.

"Well, it's not every year you get a gift like you did from your brothers."

His lips brushed her hair, his breath warm and light. "That helped, but it had nothing to do with Christmas. It would've happened no matter what time of year it was. No, it's you, Denise. It's all you. Decorating the trees, which I hadn't bothered with for, well, forever. Taking drives to see the decorations. At this time of year I'm usually scrounging for things to do to keep busy. I chop firewood. I cook a lot and stock my freezer. I read. I haven't done any of that this time."

She angled back to look at him, appreciating his honesty, and adding her own. "Mine haven't been great, either, especially since I haven't shared it with family since I moved to Sacramento, not on the actual day, anyway. I've loved every minute of it with you." *I love you.*

He brushed her hair from her face. "I'm glad you're here."

"Me, too."

His lips touched hers, brushing lightly back and forth. She sighed.

"How would you like a foot rub?" he asked against her mouth. "Let me return the favor."

Actually, she just wanted to go straight to bed. She'd been so aroused for so long that she just wanted to get it over with. *Then* they could slow down.

"That sounds wonderful," she said instead.

He propped some pillows for her to put her head on. She started to kick off her shoes, but he stopped her. "I'll do that."

She gave in to his fantasy, deciding to let him take charge. They were going to end up where she wanted, anyway, so she stretched out and put her feet in his lap, the action making her skirt ride up so that the tips of her garters showed. She watched him take notice then she closed her eyes, wanting only to feel.

His thighs tightened beneath her calves. After a minute he took off her shoes and pressed his thumbs into her arches, making her suck in a breath.

"Too hard?" he asked, his voice hushed.

She shifted a little. When had her arches become erogenous zones, anyway? "No. You have great hands."

He worked her feet until she groaned.

"I should stoke up the fire," he said. "It's dying."

"My fire is completely stoked, mountain man. Don't go anywhere."

He laughed, a deep, velvety sound. "It'll just take a second."

She rose on her elbows to watch him. The fire flared when he poked it, spitting tiny sparks, illuminating him, the light creating fascinating shadows. Everything about him appealed to her, called out to her.

He pulled off his sweater and tossed it aside as he walked back, then his tee shirt. He'd taken his boots off earlier. Now he was dressed only in black jeans, the firelight playing on his bare chest.

He knelt between her feet on the sofa, ran his hands up her legs and unhooked her garters. She squirmed and closed her eyes.

"Don't," he said. "Watch. Enjoy."

She remembered thinking before that he would know how to please, that he would give every experience his whole effort. He was proving it, taking his time, making it memorable.

She watched him peel off her stockings, letting them drift onto the coffee table. He ran his hands up and down her legs—up the outside, down the tops, back up the insides, his fingers sliding all the way to the top, his fingertips pressing lightly against her underwear then back down again. He lifted her feet to rest against his bare stomach, which felt like a sheet of hot steel. Her gaze locking with his, she slid a foot down to cover his fly, and watched his jaw harden, his eyes close to slits. She rotated her foot, heard him draw a quick breath through his teeth.

Spellbound, she sat up, her legs draped over his thighs, and put her hands on his strong, broad chest. She leaned forward and licked the spot over his sternum, letting her hands discover him, feeling every muscled ridge. His head dropped back. He groaned. Then she unbuttoned his jeans, worked at getting the zipper down, and freed him.

"No underwear," she said, surprised, but taking him into her hands, savoring the hot, smooth length of him. "How daring."

She bent low, swirled her tongue over him, felt his whole body go rigid as he let out a sound that encouraged and aroused her even more. She felt wicked, in the best way imaginable. She wanted to do things she'd never done before, had never wanted to do before.

"Denise." He tugged on her hair, moving her back, making her look up at him. "Let's go to bed. I want space. Lots of it."

Hand in hand, they went. She turned to face him, dancing backward, letting him see her pleasure at being with him, stopping to kiss every few steps, unable not to. He turned on a light and threw back the bedding, leaving the whole, huge expanse of bed. He shoved his jeans down and off.

"I've never seen anything more perfect in my life," she said, awed. Statues could be carved of his body and spotlighted on museum pedestals for centuries.

He came toward her, everything about him hard with arousal. And yet his hands were gentle as he unzipped her dress and let it drop to the floor. His hair grazed her body as he bent to pick up the dress and lay it on the nightstand. Then he reached around her to unhook her garter belt, their abdomens pressed together. He pulled the garter belt from between them and tossed it onto her dress, leaving her in her Christmas-red corset and thong.

"You don't know the nights I've laid awake, fantasizing about this moment," he said, his voice rough. "You don't know what it took for me not to go to you in the dark of night, knowing you slept naked, knowing how much I wanted you, had wanted you since you first walked into the bar during Valerie's bachelorette party."

He was saying all the right things. "I felt the same."

"I could tell."

She smiled. From someone else it might sound like boasting, but she knew he was just being honest. Their attraction had been mutual and instantaneous. It was why she'd tried to leave the wedding early and not dance with him. She was afraid of her response to him, knew he would somehow interfere with her plans, her schedule. Change her life.

He took his time unhooking her corset, using his fingers and mouth to soothe and arouse as he went. When the final hook was undone and the corset popped free, he covered her breasts with his hands, ran his fingers down the indentations the garment left behind, rubbing at the imprinted skin, then moving to her nipples, hard and aching for him to touch and taste.

She didn't try to control her response, but let her reaction come freely and her hands move over him, tug at him, dig into him, as he licked her nipples, then drew them into his mouth, sucking, nibbling, sending her soaring.

Less controlled now, he grabbed her thong and pulled it down her legs. "Now, *this* is perfection," he said, standing back, admiring her, bringing tears to her eyes. No one had ever called her that.

He urged her to lie down then stretched out beside her. "I can't touch much of you this way," she said, wanting to also roll to her side, give herself free access to him.

"If you touch me, I won't be of any use to you. I have things I want to do first. You gonna complain about that?"

"Absolutely not."

"Okay, then. Relax. Enjoy it."

"I can't promise to relax."

He laughed, low and sexy, as he started running his hands over her, then his fingers, then his fingertips, murmuring to her in erotic detail how she felt to him and what he liked about her body, making her keep her eyes open, taking her hand now and then, moving it with his to feel her own body, something she'd never done during lovemaking, having her show him what she liked.

This was the adventurer she'd wondered about, the man who knew how to please, who gave his all to every experience.

She liked everything he did. Everything he said. Everywhere he touched. He was incredibly gentle and generous. She climaxed once from the long, soft, gliding strokes of his fingers, then again from his clever, teasing mouth, then he finally covered her body with his and thrust into her, filling her with his power and heat. She grabbed tight, arched high and exploded in a climax that seemed to last forever. He rose above her, met her gaze, his forehead beaded with sweat, his muscles bulging. She wrapped her legs higher around him. His teeth clenched, a long, loud sound came from his throat and echoed in the room, flattering her, pleasing her. He moved in strong rhythm, then pressed forward, stopping, his face contorted. Then ever so slowly, ever so gently, he blanketed her body with his.

She wept at the beauty of it all.

Gideon looked over at the clock. It was 2:00 a.m. Denise was sound asleep pressed tightly against him, her legs entwined with his. His body was heavy with satisfaction and exhaustion, but his mind was firing on cylinders he didn't know he had.

She was, quite simply, phenomenal.

Why had she come along when he had no time to give her? Or to discover if what they had could be more? She'd said before that she wasn't high maintenance, that maybe she could be happy taking what she could get. He'd never known anyone who could stick to that. They think they can handle it, but they get tired of waiting. A human condition.

If the Bakers accepted his offer, he would hit the ground running the very next day. He had a business plan in place, and bids for certain elements of the resort, but he would need staff and consultants, permits to obtain. Would need more than twenty-four hours a day, so that they could break ground for the hotel right after snow season.

But first he needed to decide who to partner with, not an easy decision, and part of the reason why he was awake now, as his answer kept changing.

He also needed to convince Jake McCoy to take over his business for now so that he could concentrate on what else he needed to do, without losing what would be an important part of the overall business.

But before all that he needed to make love to the beautiful woman in his arms again. Now. They'd taken a shower together a couple of hours ago, and she still smelled like his soap.

He buried his face in her hair, toyed with the long, soft tresses that lay on his chest.

"Your brain's working so hard, it woke mine up," she said, all warm and sleepy. She cozied herself up a little more. "You should be worn out."

"One would think." In fact, he felt energized.

"I know exactly how to put you to sleep," she said, angling back.

"Warm milk?"

"No."

"A lullaby?"

"Trust me, you wouldn't want me to sing to you."

He couldn't take his eyes off her, she was so incredibly beautiful. "Tell me."

"A massage."

A massage? Was that all? He didn't want to seem

unappreciative, however, so he said, "That would be nice."

She laughed. "That was the most lukewarm sentence I've ever heard you utter." She flipped back the covers and told him to roll over. "I can guarantee you you've never had a massage like this one."

A long time later, he had to agree with her. Pleasantly exhausted and thoroughly pleasured, he closed his eyes as she leaned on an elbow, stroking his forehead with a feathery touch back and forth....

The next thing he knew daylight streamed through the windows. She wasn't in his arms but sitting cross-legged on his bed, wearing his robe, apparently just watching him sleep. Her lapels gapped, giving him a tempting view of cleavage.

"Good morning," he said, dragging himself up, leaning against the headboard.

"Good morning."

"You look like the proverbial cat who ate the canary."

"It's snowing."

"No kidding?" He craned his neck, could see flakes drifting down. Snow was rare in Chance City.

"You said you'd take me snowmobiling."

Challenge was in her eyes. He guessed she'd want her own snowmobile, not ride on the back of his, and that she'd want to race him. "Can we have breakfast first?" he asked, tugging on her bare toes.

"Sure."

He grabbed her feet and pulled her toward him. She shrieked a little as she fell flat on her back. He parted the robe and ran his hands up her thighs. "I think I'd like to return your favor first. You were right. I've never had a massage like that one. Let's see if I can make you quiver, too."

"Go for it, mountain man. I'm all yours."

I'm all yours. Her words stayed with him the whole day.

Chapter Fifteen

Most of the snow hadn't stuck to the ground. They spent the day thirty miles away in an open, snow-filled field, with flakes falling off and on. Once Denise got the hang of driving the snowmobile she was game for the challenge. She never got it up to the same speed as Gideon, but she felt like she was flying across the expanse. She'd had fun.

She'd also made a decision.

After dinner she took the wrapped package from her suitcase and gave it to him then knelt beside him on the couch. Nerves made her heart pound in her ears and a lump form in her throat.

He looked at the box, then frowned. "I didn't get you a gift."

"It's not really a Christmas gift. I just wanted a kind of ta-da moment."

He studied her face. "I don't think I want to open it."

"Why not?"

"Because whatever's in here has you spooked, big time."

She shook her head. "Excited. Big time."

As with his brothers' package the night before, he found a typed document inside layers of tissue paper, although only one page. "What's this?"

"One more option for you."

He started reading then suddenly looked up. "You? You're offering a partnership?"

"Yes." She'd changed her mind about having a silent partner, deciding that Gideon would have eliminated it out of hand, would never associate with someone he didn't know, and she couldn't introduce them. It would seem controlling, as Trevor had explained to her. She, however, was a known.

And after last night, an even better known.

"I don't understand," he said.

"I think it's pretty straightforward. I want to go in with you on the deal for The Trails."

He gave her a long, blank stare then pushed himself up off the sofa and walked to the sliding glass doors, his hands stuffed in his back pockets, and stared into the darkness. "You didn't think the choices I already had were good enough? They all committed to the necessary cost."

"When the idea came to me, no one else *had* committed to it. I planned to be your fallback. Then I realized I wanted to be involved, to see it through." She came up beside him. "I debated a lot, but I kept coming back to the same reasoning—I wanted you to have every possible option. You have Gabe Marquez, who is not family, but who wants fifty-fifty, who says he won't micromanage, but how do you know that? He already wanted changes in the contract, right? If it was *your* money on the line, wouldn't you step in if you saw even an inkling of a problem? I doubt Gabe could follow through on his best intentions."

He didn't respond, so she went on. "And then you have your brothers, who are family, who also want fifty-fifty as a single block, and that worries you, plus you already said they'll probably interfere. And now there's also me. And I'm giving you the option of a fifty-one/forty-nine split, with you retaining controlling interest. You'd call the shots."

He sort of laughed. "Right. Like you'd turn over any reins. You have a vision, too."

"Which I already shared with you. Gideon, I've already built a business. I've realized my dream. I know how good that feels. I want you to know how that feels, too."

"How altruistic of you."

His coldness cut into her excitement and renewed her doubts, the ones that had simmered before reaching her decision. "That's what friendship is, Gideon. It's about wanting the best for someone, and helping that someone make a dream come true, if it's within your reach. It was within mine."

"I really can't see you taking a back seat."

"I can. It would be your project, all the way," she said, seeing his jaw twitch. "Would I like to have input? Yes. But that's all."

"Did it even occur to you that I've built a business from scratch, too? Not as big as what I have planned for The Trails, but I did it. Worked hard for it. And no one helped me."

He was right. It hadn't occurred to her. Maybe because she'd never seen him in action. "You're right. I'm sorry."

He crossed his arms. "Is that document what was in the envelope your brother brought to you the other day?"

"He brought a contract that I ended up tossing. I wrote this myself because my lawyer's out of town. Technically I suppose it's not legal, but it's binding to me, and it will take only a day to make it official, as soon as he's back in his office."

"Is your father involved in this in any way?"

"No. Neither are my mother or brother or anyone else. Just me."

"You have this kind of money?"

"Yes. In a trust from my grandparents."

"If you had it all along, why didn't you build your own hotel before?"

"Fear of failure," she said honestly, opening up. She put a hand on his arm. "But I believe in this project. I believe in you."

"I really don't get it, Denise. I already had two offers. Both are good. I didn't need a fallback. You shouldn't have even offered."

"My offer is different."

"Slightly. But here's the deal—even if I hadn't gotten the others, I wouldn't have accepted yours."

Hurt pierced her heart and spread like liquid fire through her. "Why not?"

"Because it's not smart business." He shoved his hands through his hair, sloughing off her hand at the same time. "Why did you do it? Why did you decide to *complicate* my life?"

"That certainly wasn't my goal. Anyway, it may complicate your life briefly, until you decide which option is best for you, and then the complications will end."

"And you'd be fine with me choosing Gabe or my brothers?"

She hesitated.

He jumped on that. "See? Remember telling me what your brother said about the difference between nurturing and controlling?"

"I didn't say I didn't want to be involved. I said you'd always be the one with the final word."

"But this ties us up for life."

"So?"

"So, I would be obligated to you," he went on. "I can't be obligated to you, not like that. Denise, you've just put me in the biggest bind I've ever been in, personally or professionally. You're usually so clear headed. What were you thinking?"

The words just came out. "That I love you," she said quietly, clearly, and absolutely, her gaze direct, her chin up.

The longest silence in history followed, then he said, "I don't even know what to say to that."

"I guess the fact you don't says everything." She turned away, walked back to where he'd left the document and ripped it in half, uncomplicating his life. Then she went into his bedroom and packed her bag. All the mistakes she'd made in her entire life combined wouldn't add up to the magnitude of this one mistake, the resulting damage. She'd embarrassed him—with her offer and then with her expression of love. She wouldn't stay any longer. There was nothing left to say.

He hadn't moved from his place in front of the slider. She stopped beside him, set down her suitcase, pulled off her wedding ring and handed it to him. He took it without looking at her.

"I'm so sorry," she said, tears clogging her throat. "I never meant to complicate your life."

She needed to get away before she broke down in front of him, making everything a thousand times more embarrassing.

She hurried to her car and climbed in. She had no business being on the road, not with her eyes blurred with tears and her heart breaking, the pain as physical as it was emotional, but she couldn't wait for that to pass, either, so she drove off, not even looking in her rearview mirror.

Stupid. You were so stupid telling him that, she thought, chewing herself out for miles. Everyone knows you're supposed to wait for the man to say it first so that you don't look like a fool—or he doesn't feel trapped and stop calling. She'd broken a cardinal rule.

But, hey, she'd broken so many rules with him already. What was one more?

She checked to make sure her cell phone was turned on. It was. He didn't call and ask her to come back. At her condo, no phone messages from him waited. No e-mails, either.

She stood in the middle of her living room. She couldn't look anywhere and not see a remembrance of him. The little Christmas tree, her gift to him. The larger one, his gift to her. A stack of pages about Nevada incorporation law that he'd been studying, left on the coffee table. Quart containers of soups and stews in her freezer. His favorite dark ale in the refrigerator.

She wandered into the guest room. As he'd promised, it was spotless, the result of Noah's training as they grew up.

Denise grabbed a pillow from the bed and pressed her face into it, into the light, lingering scent of him. How could she have messed up so much? He had a schedule he was determined to stick to. She knew it was too soon.

She didn't regret making him the partnership offer. She truly believed he deserved to consider every available option. But telling him she loved him? Big mistake. Relationship-ending mistake.

Her phone rang, startling her. She picked up the guest room extension and said hello, trying to sound normal.

"I just wanted to make sure you got home okay."

She squeezed the receiver. "Safe and sound."

"Okay. Bye."

A beat passed. "Goodbye, Gideon."

He hung up. After a while, so did she.

Now what? She couldn't call a girlfriend. Everyone either thought she was married or they didn't have a clue. There was no one she could tell the truth to, be honest with. Someone who wouldn't judge her. Who would love her, no matter what.

Or was there?

She stared at the phone for a few seconds, then picked it up, dialed and waited for the connection, her body starting to shake, a flood of emotion ready to break the dam of containment she'd gotten so good at for so many years.

She managed to get one word out. "Mom?"

Chapter Sixteen

Gideon climbed the steps to The Trails' headquarters at noon on New Year's Eve. In the week since Christmas, more snow had fallen, was still falling. The parking lot was almost full, and as he entered the building, he saw people milling around, hot drinks in their hands, their cheeks wind-reddened. Cross-country skiers were a rigorous bunch.

A memory crept in of Denise racing up the snowbank to greet him on the snowmobile. He shoved the memory aside, as he had the others all during the week.

"Hello, Gideon. Where's your lovely bride?" Joanne Baker asked from across the counter.

"She couldn't make it. She sends her best." A pat answer and bitter lie.

"You didn't have to bring your bid in person, you know."

"I like being here." It was true, but he hoped she also heard in his answer that he was the right person to sell to.

"Let me get Ed," she said, walking away.

He stood at a window and watched a few skiers head out and some coming back in, pushing themselves along, gliding smoothly.

"Want to strap on some equipment and go commune with Mother Nature?" Ed said from behind him.

"It's tempting." Gideon turned around and made himself smile. "Hi, Ed."

They shook hands. "You're looking a little peaked," Ed said. "You catch that flu bug going around?"

He'd caught something, all right. "No. I've had a lot of time on my hands this week, so I entertained my nieces and nephews quite a bit."

"Yep. That'll do it, especially if you're not used to it. Come on in to the conference room. Joanne's getting some coffee and cookies."

He couldn't eat a thing, but he didn't say so. Nor did he say, "It's only my whole future at stake here, so why hurry?" the way he wanted to. It wasn't the Bakers' style to rush anything. They might as well have invented the saying about stopping to smell the roses.

"Did Denise take the week off, too?" Ed asked.

"She went to visit her family." That much he knew because Denise had sent him an e-mail to give him a heads up, not wanting him caught unawares. The note was all business, just as their arrangement had started.

"How come you didn't go with her, if you had so much time on your hands?"

Damn it. His head wasn't in the game today. Lies upon lies. "She only went for a couple of days. They've got a family tradition about going to the Rose Parade every year."

"Not your thing, I gather?"

"Not really."

"Son, let me give you a piece of unsolicited advice, if I may."

"Okay."

"Sometimes you just need to bite the bullet and do what your wife wants, even if it's the last thing on earth you want to be caught dead doing. It'll make her happy and appreciative, you know what I mean?" He winked. "Better all around for the both of you."

Gideon laughed, the first good laugh he'd had all week. "I'll remember that, Ed, thanks."

"Don't you tell Joanne I said so. She thinks I like going to bed-and-breakfast places. Shh. Here she comes."

"I'm sorry Denise isn't here," Joanne said as she set a tray on the table. "We had such a nice talk the last time." She gave him a look designed to ascertain whether he knew about their conversation.

"Denise said the same."

"Well, she made it very clear you are a man of morals and ethics. Those are the exact words she used. She wanted to make sure Ed and I knew that."

So that was how Denise had handled it. She hadn't gone into detail except to say she'd tried to explain to them how much she had changed, not what kind of man he was. It was so like her to protect him. Especially since he'd been the perpetrator of the lie, which wasn't exactly moral or ethical, just a man seeking a means to an end.

"What'd you think when you met the famous Deni?" Ed asked.

"That she was beautiful and smart, and I didn't want to let her out of my sight."

"Good answer."

"It's the truth." He was tempted to come clean with them, then he decided it would serve no purpose except to relieve his guilty conscience and probably knock himself out of the running. They wouldn't understand how much he wanted this, needed this. All they wanted was a good caretaker of what they'd built.

And a hefty amount of money, of course.

He slid an envelope across the table between Ed and Joanne, not knowing who would be the one to open it, not wanting to offend either of them by guessing wrong.

Ed flattened a hand on the envelope. "We debated whether to tell you...."

Gideon's throat closed, his stomach knotted, his pulse thundered. Now what?

"We were faxed an offer this morning from someone we expected would be submitting, and then later we got a call to expect one more before five o'clock tonight. I don't know where your bid stands in comparison to the others, but opening it now does no good, since we don't have them all in yet."

A new one today? That seemed suspicious to Gideon. Who? Why so late?

"So, you have three options," he said. He'd had three options, too, each one slightly different from the other, enough to have to weigh them carefully for their merits and drawbacks.

"It surprised the heck out of us." Ed smiled at Joanne, who nodded.

"When will you give us your decision?"

"When we reach it. I doubt it'll be more than a week. As you know, it wasn't solely about money for us until recently, but we've calmed down about that, too. We want it to be right. We think you know that we like to take our time, not to have any regrets."

He wished he'd taken his time with Denise, too, that he hadn't reacted as quickly and strongly as he had. Ed and Joanne were good examples of the well-lived life, moderation in all things.

"However it turns out," Gideon said, "I'm glad we met, and I hope your retirement is everything you want it to be. I admire you both very much. Frankly, I've rarely seen a couple who could work *and* play together. You're the gold standard."

He stood and extended his hand. "Thank you for the opportunity."

"Please tell Denise hello for us," Joanne said.

Ed walked him to the front door. "If you'd like to take one of the snowmobiles out for a ride, say the word. I'll arrange it."

"Word."

Ed laughed. He pulled a walkie-talkie from his pocket and got a snowmobile lined up.

"Thanks," Gideon said. "It's been a pleasure."

He walked to the barn where they were stored, then climbed aboard and took off. He knew where he wanted to go, where Ed had taken him before. The highest point of the entire property.

Three offers. The words swirled in his head. If he were a betting man, he'd bet one offer was connected with the architect Madigan somehow. As for the one that hadn't come in yet? Anyone's guess. Maybe even Denise.

He flew toward the top of the ridge. Would she do that? He didn't think so, but he also hadn't been in touch with her, either, except to send a "Thanks" e-mail to hers about being gone.

He shut his eyes for a second. What a jerk he'd been. He'd pretty much begged her to become part of his big scheme, his big lie, which she'd then participated in with grace, even when everything got complicated. And according to Gabe Marquez, *and* his own brothers, it was because of her that he'd secured the partnership offers.

He wanted this property, that hadn't changed. But even then he would be mired in lies, had involved others in those lies. Had hurt Denise. He'd also seen what it meant to have a partnership, like Ed and Joanne did, a team working toward a common goal.

The snow stopped as he reached the summit. He sat on the snowmobile looking out over the property that he wanted so much he could picture the next thirty years of his life right here, seeing parents bring their children, then those children bringing their own later.

Watching his own children grow...

Thirty years. Who did he want as a partner for all that time? He hadn't signed a contract with either Gabe or his brothers yet. And even though Denise had ripped up her letter of intent, he didn't think she would turn him down if he offered it to her. She wanted her chance to prove something to her father, to herself even more. She had the drive, the same burn that he did for success. No, more than success. Satisfaction. A need to create and see something through. To take pride in accomplishment.

I love you.

Her words fluttered in his mind, where they'd nested all week. Maybe he hadn't been completely surprised by her feelings. If he was being honest, maybe he should also admit to seeing love in her eyes for a while before she told him. He'd convinced himself she was just caught up in their situation of living together, working together, making plans, whether real or fictional. Laughing, brainstorming, cooking. Kissing. Making love.

She loved this place, too. It wasn't just an investment to her, unlike Gabe, or an investment and brotherly obligation, like Noah and David. She would be an in-your-face partner—who had good ideas. They had strengths and weaknesses that complemented each other.

But could they work together now that she'd said those words?

Exhaustion grabbed hold of him then. He was so tired. Tired of the stress, tired of worrying and wondering.

Most of all, tired of living the lie.

Denise had told Ed and Joanne that he was moral and ethical. He hadn't been either for weeks. That he'd also involved Denise in his lies? Not like him, either. He'd given himself permission to lie because he was desperate. Desperation rarely resulted in a positive outcome.

He needed to fix it, needed to take the desperation away, and he needed to do it now.

He found Ed and Joanne where he'd left them. They both looked surprised but waited for him to speak.

"I haven't been completely honest with you," he began.

* * *

Gideon found David waiting for him when he got home. He hoped his brother wasn't in need of relationship advice, because Gideon was all out of it at the moment. David and Valerie had been married for almost two months now. The honeymoon was over. David would just have to adapt.

"So?" David asked as Gideon unlocked his front door. "Did you get the bid in?"

"Yep." He lit the readied fire and grabbed a couple of beers from the refrigerator.

"Do I have to drag it out of you?"

"What?"

David sighed. "Who won the lottery to be your partner?"

"Oh. I'll tell you if my offer is accepted." He opened the bottles and passed one to his younger brother, who, after a moment, held his out toward Gideon.

"Are we toasting something?" Gideon asked.

"We are."

Gideon knew then, even before David announced, "I'm going to be a father. Me. The one who said he'd never get married. I couldn't love Hannah more if I'd provided the DNA, but I missed the baby stage. Is that crazy to admit?"

No. Gideon completely understood. "You'll be a great father, just like Noah. He was determined not to be anything like Dad, who was a prime example of how not to parent."

"You got that right."

They clinked bottles, then Gideon gave his brother a big hug. "May you only have to change wet diapers."

David laughed and took a swig.

"You didn't waste any time," Gideon said, moving to the living room to stoke the fire, as David meandered behind him, still on his cloud nine.

"Had fun, too." He grinned. "We were going to wait a couple of years, give ourselves time to settle into marriage first, but Mother Nature had other ideas, I guess."

"You didn't plan it?"

"No. Although we weren't overly careful, either. Did you know that half of pregnancies aren't planned? We looked it up."

Gideon remembered Denise telling him about Ben and Leslie O'Keefe, how she'd gotten pregnant out of wedlock twice. "Valerie told me to ask you about setting a date for a reception for you and Denise now that the holidays are about over. Where is she, anyway?"

Gideon didn't turn around, just continued to stab at a log. "She's visiting her parents in L.A."

"Seems like you'd want to spend New Year's Eve together."

"Of course, but I needed to be here to present the offer, and she needed to be there for some family event."

David sat on the sofa. "Have you met her family?"

"Just her brother, Trevor."

"You haven't met her parents? How'd you manage that?"

"We haven't told them we're married yet."

David went silent for a few beats. "How come?"

"Timing." Gideon set the poker in the tool stand, then sat with his brother.

"Do you miss her?"

He hesitated. "Yeah. I do."

"When will she be back?"

"I don't know for sure. She can work from down there for a while, if she needs to."

"Well, maybe you should do something to this place to make it more welcoming for her before she gets back."

"What do you mean?"

"Look around, Gid. She's not here."

"I know. I told you—"

"No, she's not *here*. There's no sign of her. No pillows you have to move before you sit down. No flower arrangements. No knickknacks. Nothing. No Denise anywhere. Don't you think you should make her feel like she's home? Valerie had no sooner moved in when all that stuff started appearing. Plus curtains. You should think about that."

He didn't want curtains, but he knew what David meant. No, she wasn't there. Might never be *there*. Not in the way David was saying.

"I hadn't realized how...I don't know, how *sterile* my house was before," David continued. "Then, of course, there's also Hannah's stuff everywhere. And the dog's underfoot. I gotta admit, I like it."

Gideon had never heard his brother so content, even though his life was a whole lot busier now than it had ever been, at least his personal life.

Gideon almost told David the truth about Denise, about the pretend marriage, about the hurt he'd caused her when all she'd done was agree to help him out of a tricky situation. If it hadn't been for her, he wouldn't have the offers he had to choose from. And yet he hadn't been able to come up with anything to say when she told him she loved him. How much had that hurt her? Enough that she'd escaped to her parents' house, a place she'd avoided for five years.

Now that he'd had time to think about it, he realized even more how much she'd given him. And in return, what had he given her? Nothing. Not even a response to her telling him she loved him.

It was one more thing he had to fix.

Chapter Seventeen

After spending a little more than two weeks with her family, Denise returned home. She'd stayed away as long as she could—until Stacy needed a break at the office and Denise had reached saturation point with her parents. She'd done some healing in the home where she was raised. Healing of self, and healing of her relationship with her family. But enough was enough. It was time to face the real world again.

She didn't pull into her parking space until 11:00 p.m., so she was dragging by the time she reached her condo. She put her key in the lock, turned the handle, pushed—

Then held tight, not letting the door open too far. Lights were on. Someone was humming. Humming? It sounded a lot like—

"Gideon?" she asked, opening the door farther. He was taking ornaments off the big tree.

"Welcome home," he said, continuing to remove the sparkly decorations and put them in boxes.

"How'd you get in?"

"You gave me a key. I left it on the kitchen counter, in case you want it back." He didn't look at her but continued to work.

She slid her suitcase to one side and shut the door, at the same noticing a grocery sack filled with papers, books and a few toiletries. The little tree was still decorated. So, he was only taking care of the big one, the one with his own ornaments on it? He was gathering the stuff he'd left behind, the things that had turned her home into theirs, those few items that had made their way into the house because of him.

She'd thought she would be fine seeing him again.

She wasn't.

She was scared—and also ticked off that it wasn't on her terms but his, by him being here instead of her setting the day and time for a necessary conversation.

"How'd you know I was coming home?" she asked, moving closer to him.

"Trevor."

"When did you two become buddies?"

"Since he called to chew me out for making you cry."

She would've liked to have heard that conversation. At least through all of this mess she had her brother back. "What'd you say?"

"That I'd meet him somewhere so he could test out his gut punch, if he wanted."

Was he admitting that he'd been wrong? She really didn't want to play guessing games. "Why are you here, Gideon?"

He finally looked at her. "I was thinking about a discussion I had with David last week. He looked around my place and said there were no signs of you, as if you didn't exist. Which is true, isn't it?"

"I guess so. I never moved in, though, so why should there be?"

"Exactly."

She waited for him to continue, but he didn't. "And so the answer to why are you here is?" she asked.

"It reminded me that there was a little bit of me here—my ornaments. And then it occurred to me that the trees might still be up, and that was a fire danger. Plus it was long past our scheduled time to undecorate."

Confused, she joined him at the tree, trying to find logic in what he'd said. If she didn't know better, she would think he was also scared. Or something. It wasn't like him to avoid eye contact.

They worked in silence. She didn't even turn on music or the television, the loud, horrible sound of no sound surrounding them, so that she could hear her heart beating like crazy, not letting up.

Finally, he'd stored her Christmas boxes, put his own next to the grocery bag by the front door then dragged both trees downstairs to the big garbage bins. She had most of the garland down by the time he got back. Another ten minutes and the house was free of Christmas.

She stood in the middle of the living room. It had never looked so stark and empty—just like she felt. Was that his point? That his place was empty of her, and so her place should be empty of him? Everything equal?

Why wasn't he talking to her? She didn't want to be

the one to carry the conversation. She had too much to tell him and didn't even know where to start.

I told you I love you and you said you didn't know what to say.

She thought she'd come to terms with that. No one could make someone love them. Just because she'd fallen for him didn't mean he felt the same, could *ever* feel the same. She'd accepted that—until this morning.

"How are you?" he asked, keeping his distance.

"Just dandy."

He reacted to her curt tone with a soothing one. "Can I fix you some tea?"

The caretaker in him apparently never died. "No, thank you." She sat in a chair and set her hands in her lap.

"I understand you telecommuted," he said, taking a seat on the sofa.

"Yes. Stacy did a great job. She's ready to take over." She knew her voice sounded tight. She'd wanted so much not to react to him, not to want him, not to wish she could be in his arms.

"Cecily keeps asking me what happened with the Bakers," she said. It had killed Denise not knowing what was going on, yet there was no one she could call and ask about it, because everyone else already thought she knew the answer. She was his wife, after all.

Why she'd continued to protect him, she didn't know.

No, that wasn't true. She did know.

"The Bakers took until today to decide," Gideon said. "My bid came in as the lowest."

Disappointment knocked the wind out of her. She'd

wanted it to happen, even if she wasn't part of it. Her whole life had changed because of The Trails. She at least wanted to see some rewards for all she'd been through—and would continue to go through—because of the deal.

"I'm sorry. I know how much it meant to you," she said.

"I told Ed and Joanne the truth."

It took a few seconds for his words to settle in, to make sense. "You what? Why?"

"Because I was tired of living the lie. It wasn't who I am. It had worn me down. Even worse, I took you down with me. I can't believe I'd allowed that to happen. So I told them, the same day I gave them my offer."

"What did they say?"

"They were shocked and hurt."

"I'm sure. On top of all that controversy about my reputation, too. I guess we—you never stood a chance."

"You think it was payback for the lies?" he said.

"Don't you?"

"I might have, except they accepted my offer. In the end they decided I—*we* were the best choice, even though one offer came in twenty percent higher."

We. He said *we.* She didn't know how to react, so she just kept talking. "I'm amazed that they could turn that much money down."

"Their children were the reason for the delay. They wanted their parents to take the highest bid. Ed and Joanne wanted to make everyone happy, but they went with their hearts, as Joanne said. Although they may not have if I hadn't promised them I was going to undo the lie."

"I don't understand." And she didn't want to get her hopes up.

Then he was there, crouched in front of her. Her nerve was fading fast. She needed to tell him. Instead she looked at her lap.

She felt his finger run along the chain she still wore, had never taken off since he'd put it on her the first night, even though it no longer held the ring.

What was he up to now? More torment? Keep reminding her of the moments she cherished? Why? She might have to talk to him but she didn't have to make it so easy on him, either, she decided. He was probably going to be furious, so she might as well get a few figurative swings in first. She shoved him away, but he only moved back a little, onto one knee. He locked gazes with her, looking half scared to death, half pathetic. Why?

"You haven't asked who I chose to partner with," he said.

"I'll bet it's David and Noah. Family comes first."

He pulled out a piece of paper from his back pocket and passed it to her. It was her one-page contract, the one she'd ripped up. He'd taped it back together and signed it. He'd also changed the terms to fifty-fifty.

"I don't understand," she said, brushing her hand over his signature.

"You're right. Family comes first, Denise. If that's what you want."

She almost stopped breathing. "What are you saying?"

"This is missing something," he answered, his finger grazing her skin, tugging at the necklace chain again.

"I forget it's there." Yet another lie.

He lifted it. She panicked. He was taking it back? "You don't have to take it. I'll give it back. Gladly."

He frowned. "I don't want it back. What would I do with it?"

"Keep it for your on-schedule wife, three years from now, I guess." Why had she said that, all snippy like that?

"I know I hurt you, Denise. I'm sorry. You'll never know how sorry."

She crossed her arms. "Honestly, Gideon, I don't know what to believe anymore."

"You can believe this—I told Ed and Joanne the truth. I want to turn the lie into the truth. Why are you being dense? You're never dense."

She felt her mouth drop open. Then she finally saw that he looked panicky, too. "Maybe you just need to be more direct," she said quietly, trying to calm herself as well as him.

"I'm trying to tell you I love you," he said, the words coming out like sandpaper. "That I want to be partners with you, in work and in life. I'm trying to ask you to marry me, for real this time."

"You love me?"

He framed her face with his hands. "Yeah. I do. With my whole heart."

"Since when?"

He laughed. "I don't know. Probably forever. But for sure since David told me Valerie was pregnant, and I wished it was me and you instead."

She drew a deep breath. "Hold that thought."

Denise got her purse from the kitchen counter and brought it back with her. Her hands shaking, she opened it, searched, then pulled something out. She held it up and showed him.

"That looks like a pregnancy test," he said cautiously.

"It is. And that's a plus sign you see in the window."

"Which means you're pregnant?"

"I found out this morning." She waited, needing to know how he felt about it, hadn't given him an answer to his proposal until she knew how she felt about her news.

"I thought you were on the pill."

"I was, but I didn't exactly take all the dosages correctly this month." Another way he'd disrupted her life. But she wasn't going to say she was sorry for messing up. She wasn't sorry. It wasn't the way she'd planned it for herself, but she wasn't sorry. Leslie O'Keefe would understand. "I know you must be in shock, Gideon, but—"

"You haven't answered my question. Will you marry me?"

"Yes."

"Do you love me?"

"Yes."

"Will you be my partner forever?"

"Yes. Yes, yes, yes. Are you okay with…" She held up the pregnancy test.

"Yes."

"It's not on your schedule," she said, looping her arms around his neck.

"Nor yours."

"I'm going to sell Stacy my business. I'm done."

"Talk about blowing your schedule to smithereens." He kissed her, took it long and deep. "I think we're going to make a hell of a team, Mrs. Falcon. Just like Ed and Joanne."

"The highest compliment."

"Ah, I'm wondering what your parents know. How much trouble am I in with them?"

"I didn't tell them about the lie. I wanted to. I wanted to tell my mom everything, but I just couldn't do that to you."

"After all the grief it caused you?"

"I guess a part of me still hoped, and I didn't want my parents to have negative thoughts about you from the beginning. It's so hard when you have to earn respect."

"Like they're not going to be annoyed with me for getting you pregnant?"

"As we said before, it takes two to tango." She kissed him, not wanting to talk anymore, just wanting to hold and be held, to kiss and be kissed. To make love freely and forever.

Catching on right away, he took her by the hand and led her to her bedroom. "I've been wanting to try out your bed."

"I never would've guessed that."

Next to her bed, he undressed her like a belated Christmas gift, one he'd gotten a rain check for before but now got to pick up and take home. Delayed gratification. It was all the sweeter. "What kind of wedding are we talking about?" he asked as he pressed kisses to her jaw.

She shivered. "An elegant one. I want the fantasy. I always have."

"But it won't take too long to put together, right?" He had her naked now, his hand pressed against her belly.

"No, not too long. My mom and I have been planning it for years."

He laughed low. "I'm just a placeholder, I guess. I suppose I'll have to wear a tux and bow tie. And shoes."

"I'll give you a foot rub after." She started undressing him, her own present to herself. "You'll look much better than my dog Toby in your bow tie."

"Small blessings," he said, then leaned down and pressed his lips to her abdomen. "I didn't know you could tell this early that you're pregnant."

"Not always. I got lucky."

He stood, drawing her close. "I'm the lucky one."

"Okay." She smiled, happy beyond measure, beyond words. She'd taken the biggest risk of her life by agreeing to become his pretend wife. She'd had to be less than truthful to a lot of people, even those she cared about most. But she wouldn't change a thing.

She'd tossed away her schedule for good.

* * * * *

Here is a sneak preview of
A STONE CREEK CHRISTMAS,
the latest in Linda Lael Miller's acclaimed
McKETTRICK *series.*

A lonely horse brought vet Olivia O'Ballivan to
Tanner Quinn's farm, but it's the rancher's love
that might cause her to stay.

A STONE CREEK CHRISTMAS
Available December 2008
from Silhouette Special Edition

Tanner heard the rig roll in around sunset. Smiling, he wandered to the window. Watched as Olivia O'Ballivan climbed out of her Suburban, flung one defiant glance toward the house and started for the barn, the golden retriever trotting along behind her.

Taking his coat and hat down from the peg next to the back door, he put them on and went outside. He was used to being alone, even liked it, but keeping company with Doc O'Ballivan, bristly though she sometimes was, would provide a welcome diversion.

He gave her time to reach the horse Butterpie's stall, then walked into the barn.

The golden retriever came to greet him, all wagging tail and melting brown eyes, and he bent to stroke her soft, sturdy back. "Hey, there, dog," he said.

Sure enough, Olivia was in the stall, brushing Butterpie down and talking to her in a soft, soothing voice that touched something private inside Tanner and made him want to turn on one heel and beat it back to the house.

He'd be damned if he'd do it, though.

This was *his* ranch, *his* barn. Well-intentioned as she was, *Olivia* was the trespasser here, not him.

"She's still very upset," Olivia told him, without turning to look at him or slowing down with the brush.

Shiloh, always an easy horse to get along with, stood contentedly in his own stall, munching away on the feed Tanner had given him earlier. Butterpie, he noted, hadn't touched her supper as far as he could tell.

"Do you know anything at all about horses, Mr. Quinn?" Olivia asked.

He leaned against the stall door, the way he had the day before, and grinned. He'd practically been raised on horseback; he and Tessa had grown up on their grandmother's farm in the Texas hill country, after their folks divorced and went their separate ways, both of them too busy to bother with a couple of kids. "A few things," he said. "And I mean to call you Olivia, so you might as well return the favor and address me by my first name."

He watched as she took that in, dealt with it, decided on an approach. He'd have to wait and see what that turned out to be, but he didn't mind. It was a pleasure just watching Olivia O'Ballivan grooming a horse.

"All right, *Tanner,*" she said. "This barn is a disgrace. When are you going to have the roof fixed? If it snows again, the hay will get wet and probably mold..."

He chuckled, shifted a little. He'd have a crew out there the following Monday morning to replace the roof and shore up the walls—he'd made the arrangements over a week before—but he felt no particular compunction to explain that. He was enjoying her ire too much; it made her color rise and her hair fly when she turned her head, and the faster breathing made her perfect breasts go up and down in an enticing rhythm. "What makes you so sure I'm a greenhorn?" he asked mildly, still leaning on the gate.

At last she looked straight at him, but she didn't move from Butterpie's side. "Your hat, your boots—that fancy red truck you drive. I'll bet it's customized."

Tanner grinned. Adjusted his hat. "Are you telling me real cowboys don't drive red trucks?"

"There are lots of trucks around here," she said. "Some of them are red, and some of them are new. And *all* of them are splattered with mud or manure or both."

"Maybe I ought to put in a car wash, then," he teased. "Sounds like there's a market for one. Might be a good investment."

She softened, though not significantly, and spared him a cautious half smile, full of questions she probably wouldn't ask. "There's a good car wash in Indian Rock," she informed him. "People go there. It's only forty miles."

"Oh," he said with just a hint of mockery. "*Only* forty miles. Well, then. Guess I'd better dirty up my truck if I want to be taken seriously in these here parts. Scuff up my boots a bit, too, and maybe stomp on my hat a couple of times."

Her cheeks went a fetching shade of pink. "You are twisting what I said," she told him, brushing Butterpie again, her touch gentle but sure. "I meant…"

Tanner envied that little horse. Wished he had a furry hide, so he'd need brushing, too.

"You *meant* that I'm not a real cowboy," he said. "And you could be right. I've spent a lot of time on construction sites over the last few years, or in meetings where a hat and boots wouldn't be appropriate. Instead of digging out my old gear, once I decided to take this job, I just bought new."

"I bet you don't even *have* any old gear," she challenged, but she was smiling, albeit cautiously, as though she might withdraw into a disapproving frown at any second.

He took off his hat, extended it to her. "Here," he teased. "Rub that around in the muck until it suits you."

She laughed, and the sound—well, it caused a powerful and wholly unexpected shift inside him. Scared the hell out of him and, paradoxically, made him yearn to hear it again.

* * * * *

Discover how this rugged rancher's wanderlust
is tamed in time for a merry Christmas, in
A STONE CREEK CHRISTMAS.
In stores December 2008.

Silhouette®

SPECIAL EDITION™

FROM *NEW YORK TIMES* BESTSELLING AUTHOR

LINDA LAEL MILLER

A STONE CREEK CHRISTMAS

Veterinarian Olivia O'Ballivan finds the animals in Stone Creek playing Cupid between her and Tanner Quinn. Even Tanner's daughter, Sophie, is eager to play matchmaker. With everyone conspiring against them and the holiday season fast approaching, Tanner and Olivia may just get everything they want for Christmas after all!

Available December 2008
wherever books are sold.

HARLEQUIN® *Romance*.

Marry-Me Christmas

by *USA TODAY* bestselling author
SHIRLEY JUMP

A *Bride* FOR ALL *Seasons*

Ruthless and successful journalist Flynn never mixes business with pleasure. But when he's sent to write a scathing review of Samantha's bakery, her beauty and innocence catches him off guard. Has this small-town girl unlocked the city slicker's heart?

Available December 2008.

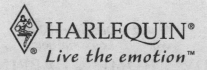

HARLEQUIN®
Live the emotion™

www.eHarlequin.com

HR17557

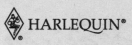

HARLEQUIN®

American ★ Romance®

HOLLY JACOBS
Once Upon a Christmas

Daniel McLean is thrilled to learn he
may be the father of Michelle Hamilton's
nephew. When Daniel starts to spend
time with Brandon and help her organize
Erie Elementary's big Christmas Fair, the
three discover a paternity test won't make
them a family, but the love they discover
just might....

**Available December 2008
wherever books are sold.**

LOVE, HOME & HAPPINESS

www.eHarlequin.com

HAR75242

THE ITALIAN'S BRIDE

Commanded—to be his wife!

Used to the finest food, clothes and women,
these immensely powerful, incredibly
good-looking and undeniably charismatic
men have only one last need: a wife!

They've chosen their bride-to-be and they'll
have her—willing or not!

Enjoy all our fantastic stories in December:

THE ITALIAN BILLIONAIRE'S SECRET LOVE-CHILD
by CATHY WILLIAMS (Book #33)

SICILIAN MILLIONAIRE, BOUGHT BRIDE
by CATHERINE SPENCER (Book #34)

BEDDED AND WEDDED FOR REVENGE
by MELANIE MILBURNE (Book #35)

THE ITALIAN'S UNWILLING WIFE
by KATHRYN ROSS (Book #36)

REQUEST YOUR FREE BOOKS!

2 FREE NOVELS PLUS 2 FREE GIFTS!

▼ Silhouette®

SPECIAL EDITION®

Life, Love and Family!

YES! Please send me 2 FREE Silhouette Special Edition® novels and my 2 FREE gifts (gifts are worth about $10). After receiving them, if I don't wish to receive any more books, I can return the shipping statement marked "cancel." If I don't cancel, I will receive 6 brand-new novels every month and be billed just $4.24 per book in the U.S. or $4.99 per book in Canada, plus 25¢ shipping and handling per book and applicable taxes, if any*. That's a savings of at least 15% off the cover price! I understand that accepting the 2 free books and gifts places me under no obligation to buy anything. I can always return a shipment and cancel at any time. Even if I never buy another book from Silhouette, the two free books and gifts are mine to keep forever.

235 SDN EEYU 335 SDN EEY6

Name _____ (PLEASE PRINT)

Address _____ Apt. #

City _____ State/Prov. _____ Zip/Postal Code

Signature (if under 18, a parent or guardian must sign)

Mail to the Silhouette Reader Service:
IN U.S.A.: P.O. Box 1867, Buffalo, NY 14240-1867
IN CANADA: P.O. Box 609, Fort Erie, Ontario L2A 5X3

Not valid to current subscribers of Silhouette Special Edition books.

Want to try two free books from another line?
Call 1-800-873-8635 or visit www.morefreebooks.com.

* Terms and prices subject to change without notice. N.Y. residents add applicable sales tax. Canadian residents will be charged applicable provincial taxes and GST. Offer not valid in Quebec. This offer is limited to one order per household. All orders subject to approval. Credit or debit balances in a customer's account(s) may be offset by any other outstanding balance owed by or to the customer. Please allow 4 to 6 weeks for delivery. Offer available while quantities last.

Your Privacy: Silhouette is committed to protecting your privacy. Our Privacy Policy is available online at www.eHarlequin.com or upon request from the Reader Service. From time to time we make our lists of customers available to reputable third parties who may have a product or service of interest to you. If you would prefer we not share your name and address, please check here. ☐

SSE08R

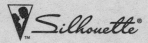

COMING NEXT MONTH

#1945 THE STRANGER AND TESSA JONES—
Christine Rimmer
Bravo Family Ties
The Bravos meet the Jones Gang as two of Christine Rimmer's
famous Special Edition families come together in one very special
book. Snowed in with an amnesiac stranger during a freak blizzard,
Tessa Jones soon finds out her guest is none other than heartbreaker
Ash Bravo. And that's when things really heat up....

#1946 PLAIN JANE AND THE PLAYBOY—Marie Ferrarella
Fortunes of Texas: Return to Red Rock
To kill time at a New Year's party, playboy Jorge Mendoza shows
the host's teenage son how to woo the ladies. The random target
of Jorge's charms: wallflower Jane Gilliam. But with one kiss
at midnight, introverted Jane turns the tables on this would-be
Casanova, as the commitment-phobe falls for her hook, line and
sinker!

#1947 COWBOY TO THE RESCUE—Stella Bagwell
Men of the West
Hired to investigate the mysterious death of the Sandbur Ranch
matriarch's late husband, private investigator Christina Logan enlists
the help of cowboy-to-the-core Lex Saddler, Sandbur's youngest—
and singlest—scion. Together, they find the truth...and each other.

#1948 REINING IN THE RANCHER—Karen Templeton
Wed in the West
Horse breeder Johnny Griego is blindsided by the news—both his
ex-girlfriend Thea Benedict *and* his teenage daughter are pregnant.
Never one to shirk responsibility, Johnny does the right thing and
proposes to Thea. But Thea wants happily-ever-after, not a mere
marriage of convenience. Can she rein in the rancher enough to have
both?

#1949 SINGLE MOM SEEKS...—Teresa Hill
All newly divorced Lily Tanner wants is a safe, happy life with her
two adorable daughters. Until hunky FBI agent Nick Malone moves
in next door with his orphaned nephew. Now the pretty single mom's
single days just might be numbered....

#1950 I STILL DO—Christie Ridgway
During a chance reunion in Vegas, former childhood sweethearts
Will Dailey and Emily Garner let loose a little and make good on an
old pledge—to wed each other if they weren't otherwise taken by
age thirty! But in the cold light of day, the firefighter and librarian's
quickie marriage doesn't seem like such a bright idea. Would their
whim last a lifetime?

SSECNM1208BPA